As always, in memory of my dear sister, Francine.

With thanks to my Beta Readers, and especially to CS for his careful editing and patient technical help.

and

For all young women who are afraid to be too clever.

> "She opens her mouth with wisdom, and the teaching of kindness is on her tongue. She looks well to the ways of her household and does not eat the bread of idleness. Her children rise up and call her blessed; her husband also, and he praises her."
> Proverbs: 31, 26-30.

Cover art: GL Robinson, 2023.

For a FREE short story please go to my website:
https://romancenovelsbyglrobinson.com

or use the code below on your phone:

Contents

Chapter One	1
Chapter Two	11
Chapter Three	23
Chapter Four	35
Chapter Five	51
Chapter Six	61
Chapter Seven	73
Chapter Eight	87
Chapter Nine	97
Chapter Ten	115
Chapter Eleven	127
Chapter Twelve	137
Chapter Thirteen	145
Chapter Fourteen	159
Chapter Fifteen	173
Chapter Sixteen	183
Chapter Seventeen	197
Chapter Eighteen	209
Chapter Nineteen	215
A Note from the Author	223
An Excerpt from Imogen or Love and Money	225
Regency Novels by GL Robinson	229
About The Author	234
Book Group Conversation Starters	235

Chapter One

"You will move to High House at the end of the month," announced Giles de Mornay, third Earl of Tyndell. "It's the only solution."

He looked critically at the woman in front of him. She was rather above average height, but it was impossible to tell if she had a shape. Her dowdy, ill-fitting round gown in a color somewhere between grey and brown was the ugliest garb he had ever seen, and her black cap, pulled tightly over her forehead with her hair braided tightly so that not a strand escaped, was the least becoming item of headwear imaginable. She could have been anywhere between twenty and forty.

Miss Drover nodded, her head down. His lordship was not, of course, asking her opinion and it was the only solution, she supposed. "I'll tell Marianne," she said quietly. "Her father's death has been such a shock; it will be hard for her to have to leave her home as well."

If his lordship heard her comment, he ignored it. "I will send a carriage for your things," he said. "You and Marianne will travel with me in my post chaise. I trust three weeks will be long enough for you to put her affairs in order?"

"Yes, my lord," replied Miss Drover. "That will be no problem." He had made no mention of her own affairs. Presumably she was deemed not to have any.

"Good. I'll leave you to it, then. You may expect me on 30th before noon. Please make sure you are both ready. I don't like to keep my horses waiting."

With that, the Earl turned towards the door, drawing on his riding gloves and calling to Woolson, the butler, to have his curricle brought round.

The news of the death of Mr. Anthony Fairchild, Marianne's father, had hit them like a bombshell. He had died of an apoplexy while away in London. That it had occurred in the arms of his mistress was a detail which had not been conveyed to his daughter and her governess. It was true he had never been a very present father. After his young wife had died giving birth to Marianne, he had spent very little time at his country estate, preferring the lively company of London society to the staid existence in the country with his daughter. She had at first been left in the charge of a nanny, but then, five years ago when she was ten, Rosemary Drover had come to be her governess. They had become very close, with Rosemary becoming Marianne's friend and almost-mother, though the age difference between them was under ten years. It had crossed Rosemary's mind that the Earl might consider Marianne old enough to go alone and pay off her governess, but so far, thank goodness, there had been no mention of that.

To be left an orphan at fifteen was a shock for anyone, but it now also appeared Marianne was to move from the only home she had ever known, and go to live on the estate of her guardian, Lord Tyndell, her mother's older brother. Her father's estate was entailed away to a cousin who would be arriving with his family any day to take possession of his inheritance. Apparently, he was blessed with two daughters of his own, one just fourteen and the other almost twelve, and he, or more probably his wife, obviously did not want to be saddled with another girl to bring out when the time came.

Hearing the front door slam behind the departing Earl, Miss Drover left the drawing room and went slowly towards the stairs. She would have to explain to Marianne, again, how it was that they had to leave. Now they had a fixed date for their departure the time for commiseration was over and there was much to do. Fortunately, Marianne was not left penniless. She had inherited her mother's fortune, which, while not a king's ransom, was handsome enough. Unfortunately, it was to be administered by her unsmiling uncle the Earl, until she came of age, or married with his consent.

Along with the fortune, there were various household items always referred to as *her ladyship's...*, as in, for example, *her ladyship's writing desk*, which resided in the breakfast room, *her ladyship's mirror,* which hung in the hall, *her ladyship's fire screen* in front of the fire in the salon, and all the items in *her ladyship's bedchamber*. These would have to come with them when they left. In fact, thinking about it now, Rosemary realized that a carriage would hardly be sufficient for it all. She should have mentioned it, but remembering his lordship's stern assumption of control, she hardly knew when a moment would have been right to tell him anything. She would write him a letter and let him make whatever arrangements he thought suitable.

After a brief knock at the door, she went into Marianne's room. This still had the look of a child's bedchamber, with its narrow bed with gingham hangings and framed Bible texts on the walls. Indeed, her charge and she had laughed over it only recently, Marianne declaring that it was time for something more adult. At fifteen, she was a well-developed girl of no more than average height, very fair with unexpectedly deep brown eyes fringed with black lashes. Her attractiveness came as much from a vivacity of character as from her undeniably pretty face.

"After all, I shall be sixteen next year and grown up!" she had said. "I should like a huge bed, with red silk hangings, a crystal chandelier and a vast gold framed mirror. Don't you think that would be fine, Rosie, darling?"

"No, I don't, and I'm sure your Papa will not think so either! It sounds most improper!"

"Oh, stuff! And as for Papa, he will give me anything I ask for, you know he will!"

It was true. Though he rarely came to his country estate, or perhaps just because his visits were so infrequent, Marianne's father was inclined to indulge her when he did put in an appearance. When she turned her beseeching gaze upon him, he was putty in her hands. He would pat her cheek, sigh at how much she looked like her mother and give her what she asked, so long as he did not have to dig too deeply into his pockets to do so. And now he was gone, that amiable, slightly stooped figure, still showing the signs of the handsome man he had once been, before the excesses of London had raddled his face and ruined his physique.

Marianne was lying on her narrow bed, the ruffled pink and white covers a contrast to her pale cheeks and red eyes.

"Has my uncle gone at last?" she asked. "I just couldn't bear to come down. He probably thought I was entirely lacking in manners, but I just couldn't. I don't know why he should be my guardian. I don't think he even likes me!"

"Yes, he's gone. He didn't seem to mind that you weren't there, but not, I think, because he dislikes you in particular. I have the impression he doesn't care for any of us. He just gave me instructions that we are to be ready to move to High House in three weeks."

"Three weeks! I am to leave my beloved home for ever in three weeks! Oh, it is so unfair! Why should Bernard have it? He's never been here above three of four times in his life!"

She burst into tears and buried her head in her pillow. Her governess sat beside her, stroking her back, until the spasm had passed. When it was over, they were both silent for several minutes, each sunk in her own thoughts.

Rosemary Drover knew well how Marianne felt. She, too, had been forced to leave her home for ever, under even worse circumstances. Her father had been the rector of a country parish and her mother the daughter of a gentleman of ancient lineage but no money. She had never known either of her mother's parents as they had died while she was an infant. The only concrete thing she still had from them was a locket given her by her mother with pieces of their hair on either side. But she had other, more practical, reasons to be grateful to her maternal grandparents. They had made sure their daughter, Rosemary's mother, was well educated. She had learned history and geography, as well as French and passable Italian. She could write in a fine hand, draw, sew and play the pianoforte. However, while her mother's ability had never been anything but moderate on that instrument, Rosemary had inherited her grandmother's very considerable talent.

This, together with the education that her mother had passed onto her, proved to be her lifesaver. Five years before, both her parents, along with a good number of the parishioners, including a young farmer who had been paying marked attention to the rector's daughter, had succumbed to a virulent fever that had swept through the county and had died within a few days of each other. Just seventeen at the time, she had been forced not only to leave the rectory that had been her home her whole life, but also find a way to earn her keep.

Luck, if such it can be called after the disastrous experience of losing her parents and her probable future husband at one swoop, was with her. The local Squire knew Anthony Fairchild in London, and when he heard that gentleman bemoaning the fact that he had to find a governess for his ten-year-old daughter, suggested Rosemary Drover. He knew her, he said, to be a very pretty behaved young woman with no pretentions to beauty (for he did not admire her slim figure and open countenance with its fine brown-grey eyes; his taste ran to something more opulent altogether), who knew as much as any young woman might be expected to know and could, besides, play a fine tune on the piano.

The thing was arranged. Knowing that her youth would be a disadvantage, Miss Drover had put on her dowdiest gown, pulled her naturally curly abundant chestnut hair into tight braids wound over her head, covered it with a matronly cap and unbecoming black bonnet and presented herself at Fairchild Court. Her appearance had produced the desired effect. No one even asked her age and the very decided way she answered the questions put to her made her appear much older, with the result that she had been engaged on the spot.

It had, in fact, been lucky for both sides. Rosemary had found a new home and Marianne a governess who, besides actually being able teach her something, was also the daughter of a gentlewoman. She could inculcate society manners in the young lady, who was inclined to be impulsive. When Mr. Fairchild came home on his infrequent trips, he found a daughter who could make a pretty curtsey, recite a French poem charmingly, locate all the counties of England on the map, find India on the globe and play a simple tune on the piano.

If her scholarship never amounted to much more than that, it was not for want of Miss Drover's trying. She and her mother had often discussed the writings of Descartes and Pascal, and she attempted to engage Marianne similarly. However, Marianne was inclined to think that anything written over a hundred years ago must be so completely out of date that it was not worth reading. In vain did Rosemary argue the opposite. Much more to her pupil's taste was the long novel *The Mysteries of Udolpho,* left behind by a visitor and devoured by Marianne before Miss Drover had a chance to prevent it. This undesirable reading matter had, however, so entrenched itself in her charge's mind that she now sat up suddenly and said,

"Now I am just like poor Emily! I am orphaned, as she was, but instead of being forced to live with an unloved aunt, I have to go to an unloved uncle! I am sure he will try to make me marry some awful old friend of his! Oh, Rosie, dearest! You must protect me!"

In spite of the misgivings she, too, was feeling about the move, Miss Drover had to laugh. "Yes, and he will probably put you in a tower if you refuse! You will have to climb down the ivy-covered walls and escape with a handsome prince on a snow-white horse!"

When Marianne looked mutinous, she continued, "Don't be silly, my love! His lordship will probably have nothing to do with us at all, and we shall be able to carry on in our usual way. I'm sure he has much more important things to do than to imprison innocent females! I daresay we shall hardly ever see him."

But Marianne was deriving woeful satisfaction from seeing herself as the unfortunate heroine of a gothic story and nothing

Miss Drover could say would make her get up and do something more useful.

Rosemary buried her own doubts about their new life in organizing the household to receive its new master and mistress. Once it had become clear that Marianne had gone as far as she could with her schooling, apart from urging her, often unsuccessfully, to practice the piano once a day, and having her read out loud chapters from such books and articles as might improve that maiden's mind, Miss Drover had turned her energies towards the running of the home. Her mother had been a very provident housekeeper, saying that no lady should be too proud to run a comfortable home for her family. Rosemary had learned at her side. The old housekeeper at Fairchild Court had been forced to retire to a cottage on the estate when her rheumatics made it impossible to fulfill her duties, and Miss Drover had stepped in. It was she who ordered the candles, fuel and dry goods for the house, who supervised the linen cupboard and had the thinning sheets turned ends to middle, who organized the annual spring cleaning and the taking down of the dusty old draperies for a good beating. It was she who, in a word, kept Fairchild Court looking as well as a property might, that had had scarcely a groat spent on it in nearly a decade.

It is doubtful whether Mr. Fairchild ever noticed a thing. He certainly did not seem to find it amiss that it was the governess who spoke to him about the smoking chimney in the library and the need to have it swept, or who informed him that the new hay ordered for the stables had proved moldy and she had sent it back. The servants, too, became accustomed to taking their orders from Miss Drover and when Mr. Fairchild invited guests for the shooting in the autumn, were perfectly ready to do her behest in everything. She hired extra maids from the village who washed, ironed and starched all the table linens including the darned napkins for the breakfast trays and polished all the furniture and what remained of the silver until it all shone.

She now directed the footmen to remove her ladyship's possessions from where they presently stood and place them in a dry shed, protected by holland covers. She thought it best to do this before the new owners arrived so that there should be no embarrassment. This left the mistress's bedroom totally empty. The attics yielded an old bed and washstand that could be refurbished sufficiently for use, and Rosemary mended the old silk hangings as best she could, hoping the new lady of the house would not find too much to complain about. Her ladyship's desk had stood for years in the same spot in the breakfast room, which now looked odd without it, but the newcomers would not know that; likewise the fire screen would hardly be noticed by its absence. The removal of the mirror from the hall, however, left a distinct mark of its shape on the wall. She ordered the wall to be washed with a dilute chloride of lime, which did something to remove the outline but also had the effect of making that wall look lighter than the rest. As with the bedroom furniture, she just hoped that in the first flurry of arrival, no one would notice. But in this she was to be undeceived.

Chapter Two

Mildred Fairchild, the cousin's wife, could not believe her fortune in having married a man who was now to inherit a country estate and what was left of the fortune to maintain it. The daughter of a well-to-do grocer, she had grown up in a household that boasted a cook and a couple of overworked maids, and as a married lady had run her own home along the same lines. She was now to be mistress of a large home which, in addition to the help she was accustomed to, boasted two footmen and a butler. She immediately adopted the airs of a *grande dame* and infuriated her contemporaries so much by constant reference to herself as the lady of Fairchild Court, that they were heartily glad to see the back of her when at last the lumbering coach conveyed them thither. Her husband, Bernard Fairchild, was a hesitant, cowed gentleman who could never quite remember whether he had actually offered for Mildred, or whether she had simply acted as if he had until it was too late for him to withdraw. His anticipation of being Mr. Fairchild of Fairchild Court was as far removed from his wife's as possible. He was, in fact, terrified.

As the coach swept between the high wrought iron gates that due to rusty hinges hung permanently open, Miss Drover called the staff to line up to receive their new master and mistress, and directed Marianne to stand with her just inside the front door. When it drew to a halt, Woolson, the butler, stepped forward and, as Mr. Fairchild came to help his wife down, bowed with great solemnity at them both.

"Welcome to Fairchild Court, Mrs. Fairchild, Mr. Fairchild."

To the two young ladies who followed them, he bowed with slightly less solemnity, before ushering in the whole party. Marianne, propelled forward by Rosemary, curtseyed to the couple who had arrived to force her out of her home, offered them each her hand and then introduced her governess. She welcomed the two young ladies, who stood, goggle-eyed at the wide entrance hall. This was probably the finest aspect of Fairchild Court, especially in the dim light of an early spring afternoon, with a fire blazing in the wide stone hearth and branched chandeliers throwing a warm light on the rather dilapidated furnishings. Woolson then performed the introductions to the rest of the staff. Mrs. Fairchild looked at them all down her not inconsiderable nose, and her husband shuffled behind, his eyes fixed on the floor.

"You must be tired after your journey, Ma'am," said Marianne at last, using the formula taught her by Rosemary, "Would you like to lie down, or may I have tea brought into the salon?"

"Oh, I'm never tired when there's work to be done," responded Mrs. Fairchild in a very determined manner. "Which I see there must be, to judge from the shocking condition of these walls. Why, this one," pointing to the place where the mirror had recently been removed, "is positively a different color from the rest. Before I even have a sip of tea, I should like to see the rest of the house. But where is my housekeeper? No one with that duty has been presented to me."

Rosemary stepped forward. "We have no housekeeper as such, Ma'am. I have been performing those duties in recent years, since Miss Marianne's schooling has come almost to an end."

"*You*, Miss Drover?" replied the new mistress with some hauteur. "How very irregular! I cannot have a governess as my housekeeper, besides, I shall be needing you for the instruction of my girls, though I'm sure you will find them educated to a level beyond what one may find here in the country. Dear Miss Oswald, their governess, whom we unfortunately had to leave behind, was possessed of a most superior intellect."

She did not mention that Miss Oswald was nearly sixty and because of her failing eyesight, had barely opened a book in the last few years. She had declared herself unable to move away at her time of life, preferring to go and live with her sister instead.

"I think there is some misunderstanding, Ma'am," replied Rosemary swiftly. "I am to leave with Miss Marianne. She will need a chaperone and companion at her uncle's house. But if you wish to engage a housekeeper before we leave, I shall be glad to show her how we go on."

Mrs. Fairchild sniffed and said nothing, but allowed herself to be led upstairs by Rosemary. The two girls trailed behind. Meanwhile, Marianne led Mr. Fairchild into the salon, where she invited him to sit by the fire and ask Woolson to bring him whatever he might desire. She then spent a difficult hour trying to converse with a man who had no conversation, no opinion and no social manners. All of Rosemary's training was put to the test as Marianne tried to find one subject after another that might elicit more than, "I really could not say," or "I shall have to ask Mrs. Fairchild."

Rosemary, who had already formed a fair assessment of the new mistress of Fairchild Court, thought she had best take the bull by the horns and show her immediately the denuded bedchamber that would be hers. When Rosemary explained that her ladyship's bedchamber furniture belonged to Marianne and had been removed prior to transportation to its new home, that lady's shock and disgust found immediate expression.

"But it is not to be believed! Surely the items in the mistress's bedchamber must necessarily belong to the estate. I shall have my husband look into it at once. I cannot permit anything to be removed before investigation. It is not to be expected that the lady of the house should sleep in this old stuff! It is fit only for the bonfire!"

While Rosemary agreed that the bed and washstand were old, she found herself wanting to defend the bedlinens and hangings, which she had spent time and effort refurbishing. The colors were faded to be sure, but washed and ironed, the almost grey-pink looked quite pretty, she thought. And she had chosen the best of the lace-edged pillowslips and sheets for Mrs. Fairchild. They were thin but very fine. But Mrs. Fairchild was not to be mollified.

"I demand that the original furnishings be returned," she declared. "I shall not sleep even one night in this!"

"I'm afraid that will not be possible, Ma'am," replied Rosemary, equally firmly, and, telling nothing less than the absolute truth, added, "they have already been packed up for transportation and are no longer in the house."

Mrs. Fairchild stared at her for a minute, but as she met her gaze with perfect equanimity, the mistress evidently decided nothing more could be done for the moment. But she was not satisfied. Nor was she satisfied with the contents of the linen cupboard. Rosemary had been making do and mending ever since she had been in the house, as Marianne's father had been adamant he would not spend money on what he called "damned linens and furbelows that no man could possibly care about." The contents of the linen cupboard were consequently in sorry shape.

"I suppose you will tell me that the sheets have also been removed for Miss Marianne," said Mrs. Fairchild acidly.

"No, indeed, Ma'am," said Rosemary. "We have been sleeping on ends-to-middle sheets these last two or three years. You will find I have had the only unrepaired ones put on your and Mr. Fairchild's beds. But I'm afraid the young ladies will find theirs as uncomfortable as ours."

Since the two daughters of the house had never been allowed the luxury of unrepaired sheets, they muttered something about being accustomed to it, but their mother swiftly hushed them. The tour of the upstairs continued and was completed, with Mrs. Fairchild demanding to see every room, including those where Marianne and Rosemary slept next to the nursery. Some guardian angel had prompted Rosemary to have even the unused rooms cleaned and aired, so, though they were cold and unappealing on that afternoon now lengthening into evening, at least they were clean and did not feel damp.

The tour continued downstairs into the library, the billiard room and the breakfast room.

"From the indentations in the rug I assume something has been removed from this corner," the new mistress observed crossly, indicating the space where her ladyship's desk had stood. She looked at Rosemary, waiting for a response.

"Well, yes, as you say, Ma'am. There was a desk there that belonged to Marianne's mother and was willed to her."

"I must say, I find it very high handed of you to have removed these items without my permission," said Mrs. Fairchild icily. "I wonder how you can have come to do so."

"It was thought to be for the best, Ma'am," was all Rosemary permitted herself to say.

They passed through the hall towards the dining room and salon, with the mistress commenting unfavorably again on the state of the walls. Luckily, she did not seem to associate this with the removal of another item of her ladyship's, for which Rosemary was heartily grateful. The dining room, with its huge long oak table seating thirty, looked grand enough even for Mrs. Fairchild, who looked with approbation at the dark portraits of ancestors gracing the walls.

The family's history was not an old one, the estate having been purchased by Marianne's great grandfather after he had retired from making his fortune in the British East India Company. Although she never spoke of it, Rosemary's maternal grandfather, while impecunious, had been descended from a gentleman at the court of Queen Elizabeth, and her family was thus much older than that of her employers. Nevertheless, Mrs. Fairchild was pleased to direct her girls' attention to "our ancestors", deliberately overlooking the fact that her own lineage went no further back than to a grocer's shop.

It did not stop there. Before taking a cup of tea in the salon, the mistress declared that she would see the kitchens. Rosemary knew that the cook and kitchen maids would be in the midst of dinner preparations and tried to persuade her to delay this visit till the morrow, but to no avail. The group clattered down the back stairs and Mrs. Fairchild stalked into the kitchen just as the cook was whisking the mayonnaise for the sauce to accompany the cold trout. Anyone familiar with this operation knows it is a delicate one, and Rosemary would have not interrupted it. Not so the new mistress, who demanded to know what was going on, thereby requiring the cook to stop what she was doing, curtsey and answer as best she could, thus effectively ruining the emulsification of the eggs and oil. It was not an auspicious beginning to what would, Rosemary felt, be an uneasy relationship. The cook was a lady of decided character and unlikely to take such interruptions calmly in the future.

Mrs. Fairchild, however, dismissed her with a wave of her hand and turned her attention to the Welsh dresser which displayed the household china. The plates visible on the shelves were all chipped, a fact that Rosemary could easily have explained, since the good ones were stored in the cupboards beneath for when the master and his friends were there. The chipped china was used on a daily basis by herself and Marianne and the staff.

"This china is in an appalling condition," cried Mrs. Fairchild, her eyes flashing furiously. "No doubt the good dishes have also been removed for Miss Marianne!"

"By no means, Ma'am," replied Rosemary with great calm. "They are stored underneath and will be used for you and Mr. Fairchild, of course." She opened the doors of the cupboard and showed the stacks of plates, each carefully protected by a layer of straw.

"See that they are, and let me say," she addressed the cook and her young helper, who was regarding her with scared round eyes, "any broken china will be taken out of your wages, so watch what you are about!"

With that, she swept towards the stairs, and, with her daughters scuttling behind, rose majestically upwards.

The subsequent days brought no respite from Mrs. Fairchild's nosy interfering in every aspect of the running of the Court. She demanded the stillroom keys from Woolson and, having examined the log book which recorded the extraction of each bottle from the cellars, declared she would in future keep hold of it. The butler, who had for years taken a small glass of port at night before retiring, a fact of which Rosemary was well aware but did nothing to stop, saw his future becoming less comfortable. The new mistress spoke to the gardener who was just preparing to plant the dahlias and instructed him where to put what, when he, who had been working at the Court since he was a boy, knew better than anyone which plantings prospered best where.

With her lively sense of the ridiculous, Rosemary was amused rather than dismayed by most of this crass interference, but she knew it was only a matter of time before Mrs. Fairchild discovered where her ladyship's furniture had been stored and demanded its return. Accordingly, she wrote to the Earl both to inform him that the amount of furniture needing to be transported to High House was greater than he probably expected, and to tell him, though without much hope of intervention, that she was afraid Marianne's legacy of items from her mother might be appropriated by the new mistress of Fairchild Court.

What his lordship wrote to Mrs. Fairchild in response she would never know, but it is sure that a letter with his seal arrived and was conveyed to her at the breakfast table one morning shortly before their departure. It was just as well, since only the day before, the bedroom set, the desk, the fire screen and the mirror had been discovered under their holland covers in the outbuilding.

"So this is what you meant, Miss Drover, when you said these items were no longer in the house," had exclaimed the mistress. "Be sure your slyness has found you out! I shall need to see chapter and verse of the Will before I accept the removal of these things from the Court!"

As she perused the single page missive from his lordship, red spots appeared on Mrs. Fairchild's cheeks and she was heard to suck in her breath. When her husband asked what the matter was, she replied with an assumption of ease that it was nothing, only a kind letter from Marianne's guardian confirming certain issues. But no further reference was made to her ladyship's furniture. Indeed, she hardly spoke to either Rosemary or Marianne again until the day they left.

On 30th April, the first conveyance to arrive at Fairchild Court was a good-sized cart drawn by two huge horses. Before it could get to the front door, Rosemary, who had been watching all morning and guessed it was for the furniture, quietly directed one of the footmen to lead it directly around to the shed and help load it. She did not want Mrs. Fairchild aware of what was happening, as she would certainly have interfered or forbidden the footman to help. She had already had her and Marianne's few possessions brought down into the hall. She herself had one small trunk and Marianne a trunk, and a couple of bandboxes. Their cloaks and bonnets lay over them.

Shortly before noon, his lordship's post chaise arrived. This was a splendid shining black and gold vehicle, drawn by four black horses, their tackle brightly polished and their manes closely braided. The doors bore the Tyndell coat of arms: a black griffin, rampant on a field of gold surmounted by a series of wheatsheaves. Emblazoned beneath was the motto: *Semper Duremus Villam Atque Bello*, which Rosemary, not for nothing a scholar of the classics, was able to interpret: *From Farm to Battle We Will Always Endure*. There were a coachman and postillion in front and two grooms behind, all in full livery that bore the same crest. Marianne and Rosemary looked on in amazement, while behind them the two girls shrieked, "Mama, Mama, come and see! It must be a Prince! Does he have a glass slipper for us to try?"

"Don't be ridiculous, girls! And where is your decorum? Don't shriek like that. Anyone would think you had no upbringing at all!"

Rosemary was thinking exactly that, and, sure Marianne felt the same, she turned and gave her a conspiratorial smile. His lordship, descending from his coach, saw the smile and for the first time regarded Miss Drover with a flicker of interest. She still looked as unattractive as ever, in her shapeless brown-grey gown (could it be sackcloth?), and ill-fitting cap (did she actually *have* any hair?), but her smile had momentarily transformed her. Marianne, her flaxen curls hanging prettily behind her head, her travelling gown of amber wool enhancing her nut-brown eyes now shining with unshed tears, looked absurdly young and pretty. The Earl was not looking forward to riding over four hours with a schoolgirl and her duenna, but he consoled himself with the fact that one of them at least was nice to look at, even if she looked as if she was going to be tearful.

"My lord!" Mrs. Fairchild came bustling forward. "How kind of you to come personally to escort dear Miss Marianne to her new home. I'm sure we shall all miss her dreadfully, and Miss Drover, too, of course."

Since this lady, jealous of Marianne's prettiness beside her daughters, who had both inherited her unfortunate nose and gingery complexion, had in the last week only spoken to her to criticize, and to Miss Drover not at all, Rosemary glanced at her charge with another smile. This, too, was not lost on his lordship, who nonetheless, executed a graceful bow in the direction of Mrs. Fairchild, muttering "Madam, your most obedient." At that moment, the loaded cart appeared from behind the house.

"Our trunks are in the hall, my lord," said Miss Drover. "Perhaps…"

She led the cartman and the footmen to where their trunks and few bandboxes lay. She and Marianne caught up their cloaks and put on their bonnets. Marianne's had a fetching poke front with a feather that matched her gown and cloak, both made by Rosemary from a length of material discovered in lavender in the attics; Rosemary's was the same black shapeless one she had arrived in five years before. As the two trunks and few bandboxes were loaded, the Earl reflected that he had never travelled with women with so little luggage. His light-of-loves inevitably not only weighed down the post chaise with box upon box, but also seemed to find it necessary to turn back at least twice for items unaccountably forgotten. His mother had needed another entire carriage for her things when she went away for just a few days. These two were leaving here forever and had practically nothing. To his surprise, he experienced a momentary pang.

"But will you not stop for a light luncheon, my lord?" cried Mrs. Fairchild, much to Rosemary's astonishment, as she had heard her previously announcing to her husband that she was not going to put the household about to provide a meal for this lord, whoever he may be.

But his lordship refused. "Thank you, no. We will have to stop in two hours to change the horses and we will take something then. I do not care to keep them standing much longer, so if you are both ready…"

Rosemary and Marianne both turned and looked at Fairchild Court, silently bidding adieu to their home. They curtseyed to Mrs. Fairchild and to Mr. Fairchild, who had just emerged from the library and stood blinking like some sort of animal unaccustomed to the light, then went towards the carriage. No affectionate farewells were exchanged. His lordship handed each of them up in turn, then stepped up himself. The groom put up the steps and closed the door.

"Put 'em along, John," said the Earl. They were off.

Chapter Three

As they went through the gates with the broken hinges, both ladies turned to look at their home one last time. Marianne could not help herself. The tears she had bravely held in coursed down her cheeks. She put her head in her hands and sobbed. Rosemary drew her pupil's head onto her lap and patted her back, whispering soothing sounds, until the storm passed. Then she handed her a sensible white handkerchief, and after blowing her nose and scrubbing at her eyes, Marianne sat up and took a deep shuddering breath. She became aware of her uncle surveying her with an unreadable expression.

"I'm sorry, my lord," she said brokenly. "It's just that... that..."

She seemed about to break down again, but the Earl surprised Rosemary by saying from the other end of the carriage, without, however, his stern countenance betraying anything like a smile, "Don't apologize. I daresay I would feel like crying too if I had to live with that harridan."

"Oh, it wasn't Mrs. Fairchild," protested Marianne, "it was leaving my h...h... home." She gulped.

"I think his lordship was funning," said Rosemary. "Of course, he understands how hard it is for you to leave the place you have lived all your life."

She waited for him to confirm this, and when he remained silent, she cast him a look of such stern rebuke that it took him aback. He had, of course, been trying to make light of a depressing situation, though he now realized he had made a muff of it. But he was unaccustomed to being looked at in that way, indeed in any way other than with admiration or sycophancy. He found himself wondering again about this unprepossessing female. If that was how she was going to be, he would have to get rid of her at the earliest opportunity.

Meanwhile, Rosemary had turned back to Marianne and had begun to speak to her in a low voice.

"Come, my love, let's try to make ourselves cheerful. Let's make up a frightening story about a poor maiden forced to leave her home and," she whispered even lower, "forced to go with a wicked guardian to his dark house on the lonely moors, far from any other human habitation."

Marianne made a sound, half sob, half giggle. "But she takes her faithful abigail with her, who protects her when he tries to force his advances on her in the carriage."

"Yes, and he refuses to stop for luncheon, or to rest his poor horses, who collapse with exhaustion just as they are reaching the top of the moors."

"And they have to walk the rest of the way, carrying their trunks on their backs in the pouring rain."

They both giggled at the mental image this conjured up.

"It's dark by the time they arrive," continued Miss Drover, "and he's too miserly to have more than one candle lit, so they have to grope their way to their bedchamber in the inky blackness."

"They realize there's only one blanket on each of the beds, so they put them both on one bed and get in together for warmth, as they are still wet from the walk in the rain."

"Yes, and they fall asleep, because they're so tired, but in the middle of the night the wicked guardian comes crashing in, roaring drunk, and tries to… to…"

"But they throw the blankets over him and because he's drunk he gets tangled up in them, so they run to the door…"

"…And lock it behind them with a key that they hadn't seen before because it was on the outside,"

"And run out of the house and find their way…"

"To a cottage where a handsome young farmer lives with his aged mother."

"But really, he isn't a farmer, he's a prince, and his mother is the queen. They've been forced to live there…"

"…Because the wicked guardian's brother has usurped the throne."

"But the soldiers are still loyal to the real prince, and they ride onto the moors to find him…"

"And they bring his favorite horse, snow white, of course, and the prince takes up the beautiful maiden to carry her back to London."

"But the wicked guardian looms up out of the mists, attacks the prince, and they fight a duel."

"The wicked guardian wounds the prince in a cowardly fashion, when he is looking to calm his horse…"

"But the maiden bravely grasps his sword and runs the wicked guardian through. Then she gallops to London with the prince over the saddle in a swoon. And, oh yes, she rips up her petticoat to bind his wound."

"When they get there, they find the soldiers have driven out the usurper, and the doctor says the maiden's bandages have saved the prince's life."

"So they are married and," they both whispered in unison, **"Live happily ever after**!"

"But what about the faithful abigail?" asked Rosemary softly. "What happens to her?"

"Oh, the old queen loves her so much that she adopts her and she becomes a princess."

"Does she get a handsome husband?"

"No, but a rich old man marries her and dies, so she has his fortune and she can choose any man she wants."

This amused Rosemary so much she laughed out loud, "That sounds even better!" she said, forgetting to lower her voice.

"What sounds even better?" enquired his lordship, who had been wondering what all the whispering was about. Decidedly, he thought, young women made dreadful travelling companions, except, of course, if they were flirtatious young women of a different type altogether.

"Oh, nothing really," said Rosemary. "We were just beguiling the time with one of our favorite games, which is making up a story."

"Yes," added Marianne, and continued impetuously, "and the mistreated maiden, which is me, always marries the handsome prince. But this time we made a nice ending for Rosie, too."

"And what was the nice ending for… er… Rosie?" asked the Earl, thinking that a happy ending for someone who looked like

Miss Drover was highly improbable, and that anyone less like a *Rosie* than she would be hard to imagine.

"She marries a rich old man who dies and leaves her his fortune, so she can choose any husband she wants."

"Ah, I collect," responded his lordship, "that you both consider a fortune sufficient inducement for any man?"

Aware of the implication that she had no other inducement to offer, Rosemary replied calmly, "Without beauty, or even when there is beauty but no dowry, I should think so, yes." Then she continued, "I'm glad to say that for Marianne it is not something she will have to face, being possessed of both, but it is a harsh reality for those of us who have neither."

The Earl slightly raised one eyebrow at Rosemary's outspoken response to his question, but before he could make any further comment, their attention was caught by the chaise drawing into the yard of a very busy hostelry. The shrill cries of ostlers overlay the stamping of hooves on the cobbles and the loud demands of passengers from at least three other carriages that stood there. His lordship took no notice of any of it. Once the steps had been let down, he descended in a business-like manner from the chaise, handed down the two females and herded them (there really was no other word, thought Rosemary) into the inn. The innkeeper, beholding the Earl, immediately stopped what he was doing, bowed low, and led the small party into a quiet parlor, where a table was already laid with a meal.

"I bespoke a luncheon. Please eat immediately, I don't want to spend more than thirty minutes here. We still have a long way to go," said the Earl. Then, addressing the innkeeper who was hovering reverently at his side, "Some lemonade for the ladies, and bring me a bottle of that claret. The Médoc, not any of your other rubbish."

If the innkeeper disliked hearing the contents of his cellars referred to as *rubbish*, he said nothing but scurried away to do his lordship's bidding. The two ladies did likewise, sitting down to eat as directed. Rosemary carved a plump capon, placing some on his lordship's plate, before serving Marianne, then herself. She passed him the other dishes, but he waved them away, saying impatiently,

"Serve yourselves. I daresay you are hungry. I doubt that woman keeps a generous table. I shall wait for the wine."

Since his assessment of Mrs. Fairchild's board was chillingly accurate, and all they had been offered for breakfast was weak tea and a slice of bread and butter, the ladies were very hungry. Rosemary was pleased to see Marianne eating with good appetite, her sorrows for the moment forgotten. They both enjoyed the rather rushed meal, before leaving his lordship with his wine and repairing upstairs to one of the bedchambers with the innkeeper's wife to tidy themselves before continuing their journey. When they came down, with Miss Drover making sure it was not a minute more than a half hour since they had descended from the chaise, the Earl was waiting for them. They re-boarded the post chaise and continued their journey. His lordship offered no further comment, and the ladies murmured softly together.

It was late afternoon as they approached High House, the sun trailing its last red fingertips in the sky. After leaving London, the road had gradually risen up the slopes of the North Downs and it was easy to see why the country home of the Earls of Tyndell, situated on Westerham Heights, was thus named. The estate lands lay on either side of the road and they could see orchards where blossoms were beginning to show and newly ploughed fields stood ready for the spring planting. Rosemary thought of the sheaves on the coat of arms and imagined that in a few months the fields would be waving with golden-eared wheat. She knew this part of Kent was famous for its cider as well as for beer, and hops would soon grow wild in the hedgerows.

As they passed cottages and farmhouses, the inhabitants came outside, the men removing their caps, or touching their forelocks, the women curtseying, as they recognized the emblazoned carriage of his lordship. He occasionally waved an idle hand, but more often, ignored these salutations altogether.

When the panting horses came at last to a halt in front of High House, the front doors were flung open and a great beam of light flooded the parterre.

"So much for a single candle!" said Rosemary softly to Marianne, who nonetheless looked doubtfully at this first view of her new home.

A lean, older gentleman, whose stately demeanor proclaimed him to be the butler, hardly waited for the steps to be put down before he opened the carriage door, saying warmly, "My lord! I am so glad you are back! I hope there was no untoward incident on the road!"

"Don't be ridiculous, Anstruther. I've only been gone since this morning and I have been travelling through Kent, not the wilds of Borneo," was his lordship's chilling reply.

Rosemary hid a smile, but Marianne looked distinctly frightened at her guardian's cold response to this warm welcome. The butler, however, merely shook his head with a small smile.

Helping her out of the carriage, the Earl now said shortly, "This is my ward, Miss Marianne Fairchild, and the other lady is Miss Drover, her … her companion."

"It seems I am to have no Christian name," said Rosemary to herself. "So be it. Miss Drover I am and Miss Drover I shall remain."

But she was pleased in spite of herself to be accorded the rank of companion rather than governess. Her mother had told her about her own childhood in a gentleman's family and about the subtle ranking that went on both above and below stairs. A governess could not take meals with the family, and yet, since she was placed above the servants, she could not eat with them either. Once her charges were deemed old enough to take their place at the family table, it made for often uncomfortable solitude. A companion, on the other hand, would be seen as a member of the family, usually impoverished and little more than a fetch-and-carry person, but sitting and eating with them, and a step above a governess.

The butler came forward and confirmed Rosemary's assessment by bowing over each of their hands in turn, before ushering them through the door into a wide hall, lit by innumerable candles and warmed by an enormous fire, saying, "This is Mrs. Brown, the housekeeper. She will show you to your apartments."

They were led up the wide staircase rising gracefully from the enormous hall. Rosemary was astonished to see that, as well as being brilliantly lit by branched chandeliers placed in embrasures all the way up, it was carpeted. Their footsteps made no sound.

Going ahead of them, the housekeeper said, "Your belongings have not arrived yet, so you will not be expected to change for dinner tonight. But you will be able to refresh yourselves before dinner, which is at six. His lordship keeps early hours here in the country."

They turned right at the top of the stairs and walked down a corridor, also brilliantly lit and carpeted. Such luxury! Opening a door, Mrs. Brown led them into a bedchamber. Marianne gasped in delight. No more narrow bed and gingham hangings, nor yet the red silk hangings and huge gold mirror she had dreamed of, but a large, elegant, lady's room. The bed was full-size with an embroidered cream-colored silk cover and hangings. The tall windows were festooned in the same material. On the floor lay an Aubusson rug in pale colors. There was a pretty dressing table and in the corner a dressing screen that no doubt hid the washstand. A fire danced in the chimney piece and branched chandeliers threw light everywhere.

"Oh!" cried Marianne. "How lovely! We will be very comfortable here, won't we, Rosie?"

"But Miss Drover's room is next door," corrected Mrs. Brown. "It can be reached through here." She opened a door in the side wall and led them through.

Rosemary's room was similar in size to Marianne's, but had obviously been designed originally as the husband's room, next to his wife's. The bed hangings and draperies were of a deep golden-brown velvet and on the floor was a richly colored turkey rug. But, incongruously, the bedcover was of white lace-edged silk.

"When his lordship asked me to prepare two rooms for his ward and her companion, I chose these as they are the largest of the spare bedchambers, but, as you can see, Miss Drover, this was intended to be a man's room. We have beaten and aired the velvet and the rug, though I daresay you can still smell the cigar smoke if you put your nose to them. I replaced the bedcover with one of her late ladyship's and put a layer of lavender under your mattress, which I hope will drive away the lingering smell of tobacco. I *do* wish gentlemen could be persuaded not to smoke in the bedchambers. It is always *such* a problem. If it was their job to beat the rugs and draperies to try to get rid of the smell, they would change their ways and no mistake! Anyway, I hope you will be comfortable."

Since the room also boasted a nice sized desk and shelves filled with books, Rosemary could not have been more pleased. "It is perfect, thank you, Mrs. Brown," she said, smiling, "Thank you for what you have done. You have been most considerate."

"You're welcome, I'm sure," responded the housekeeper as they walked back into Marianne's room. "We always want our guests to be happy here at High House. Not that you are guests, of course. No doubt this will be your home until Miss Fairchild receives an offer to move elsewhere, if you catch my drift. That shouldn't be too long in coming, either, as pretty as she is." She beamed at Marianne, who blushed and muttered something incoherent. "Now, I'll send the maid up with some tea and do you have a nice little rest until dinner."

And she bustled away.

When she was gone the two women looked at each other and burst out laughing.

"Well," said Rosemary, "there go our hopes for a gloomy castle with closed mouthed servants who creep around in the dark!"

"Isn't it *lovely*," cried Marianne, running through into her own room and whirling around before collapsing on the bed. "*Dear Uncle Giles!* He must be really *nice* under that stuffy exterior!"

"Don't deceive yourself, my love," responded Rosemary, "I don't believe he had a thing to do with it besides telling Mrs. Brown to get two rooms ready. But you can thank him at dinner. It will be interesting to see what he says, especially if you call him *Dear Uncle Giles!*"

Chapter Four

The tea duly arrived, together with some small almond cakes. These were relished, for they were both hungry again. Their luncheon had been rushed and necessarily quite sparse. It had given Rosemary a pang to see a good deal of it left on the table. Their clothes still had not arrived, so apart from washing their hands and tidying their hair, there was not much they could do. Rosemary brushed out her charge's hair and arranged her ringlets becomingly. She was going to leave her own head exactly as it was, since the braids under her uncompromising cap were so tightly woven that not a hair had escaped.

"Rosie," said Marianne hesitantly, "don't you think you could take off that cap for once? It really doesn't become you, and now you are a *companion*, not a governess, you don't have to look so dreary, do you?"

"Oh, I'm quite fond of my ugly old caps after all this time," laughed Rosemary. "But I confess that wearing one tied so tightly all day has given me a headache." She undid her cap and threw it down. "But now I've got a red line all across my forehead which is even less becoming!" She reached for her cap to fasten it back on.

"But if you take out your braids and tie your hair back more loosely, it will fall a little over your forehead and cover the mark." Marianne encouraged her. "Do give it a try, Rosie, dear. After all, we are beginning a new life. You can have a new coiffure."

Whether it was because a new life did seem to call for a new look, or whether it was because of the relief to her headache from removing the tight cap, Rosemary acquiesced. She brushed out her chestnut curls, feeling the wonderful release that undoing tight braids always brings, and drew her heavy mane into a bun in the nape of her neck. Sure enough, the natural waves softened over her brow.

"Oh, Rosie, that looks *so* much nicer!" exclaimed Marianne. Even that awful dress looks better. The color is actually quite good with your hair! And did you know you have grey eyes? I always thought they were brownish, but with your hair like that they look quite grey, almost blue." She stared into the other woman's eyes.

"Brown, grey, who knows? I've never known what color they are. They seem to change with the weather."

"What fun! I'll wager that if you wore a blue gown your eyes would look quite blue too! We should try all different colors and see how they change!"

Rosemary laughed gaily. "If you can tell me where I am to find a blue gown, or any color other than the brownish grey I always wear, I shall dance a jig! That would be new, too!"

Marianne pondered for a minute. "But I have the very thing! There's that blue dress you made for me from that funny old gown that we thought must have been my grandmother's! Do you remember those stiff petticoats and those things on the sides, that had to be held out with sort of baskets tied over the hips, what were they called?"

"Panniers. Ladies used to think they were just the ticket, even if it made them have to go through doors sideways! But it did provide a nice lot of material. Anyway, what about it?"

"Well, you know it doesn't really become me. The blue is just too bright or something. When my trunk arrives, we'll look at it and see if it suits you. I don't know why we didn't think of it before!"

"Don't be silly, my love! It would be far too short for me, and anyway, I'm not wearing any blue gowns. What I have is perfectly appropriate. Come on, are you ready? It's almost six and God forbid we keep Lord Impatience waiting."

Marianne giggled. "You mean Dear Uncle Giles?"

"Yes. He always seems to be in a hurry. Tell you what, if he does turn out to be Dear Uncle Giles, I'll wear that blue dress, even if it only comes to my knees!"

They were both laughing at this image as they went down the elegant staircase. Anstruther heard them and thought how pleasant it was to hear genuine laughter in the house. The ladies – though the butler found it hard to call them such – that his lordship occasionally brought home would give a titter now and then, though shrill complaints were more common. He went to meet them both, and led them into the drawing room, where the Earl was drinking a glass of sherry before dinner.

Rosemary's first thought when she entered was what a comfortable room it was. In the huge fireplace a blazing fire cast its glow on dark wood furniture that was obviously old but polished into soft reflecting mirrors. A huge settle with red velvet cushions was in front of the fireplace, but far enough away to not feel the scorch of the fire, while to either side were velvet-cushioned armchairs with very high curved backs and arms. Tall branched chandeliers stood at either end of the mantle and on a large, darkly glowing sideboard that stood behind the settle. In one of the armchairs lounged his lordship, a small table bearing a bottle and a glass at his elbow. He rose to his feet as they came in, and coming towards them, directed them to the settle. Like them, he had not changed for dinner. He still wore the same jacket of superfine wool whose fit was evidently more for comfort than for fashion. He would not need his valet to help him into it. His boots glowed in the firelight but had no tassels or trim denoting a Tulip of the *ton*; his sober waistcoat bore no fobs or chains, his white, moderately collared shirt was not stiffly starched to the point where it gave him trouble moving his head from side to side, and his neckcloth was wound around his neck in a fashion more practical than precise. In Rosemary's previous brief encounters with him, she had avoided looking him in the face for fear he would perceive her youth and declare his ward no longer needed a governess, and she was too young to be a chaperone. In the post chaise, except for that one exchange, she had concentrated on Marianne. Even in the inn, to avoid incurring his impatience, she had looked mostly at her plate. Now, standing at ease in front of his own hearth, she saw that, except for the frown that seemed a permanent feature of his face, he was an attractive man.

If Rosemary was making a discovery, so too was the Earl. He waved them towards the settle and Marianne seated herself at one end. As Rosemary moved towards the other, her hair glowed chestnut in the firelight. Accustomed to stricter control, it had begun to spring from the knot at the back of her head and curl on the sides of her face. As Marianne had remarked, even the color of her gown looked better, though its fit was still atrocious. She looked completely shapeless but he realized she was younger than he had at first thought. And she had already been five years with Marianne. What on earth was Fairchild doing, he wondered, employing as a governess for his daughter someone who cannot have been much more than a girl herself?

Collecting himself and apparently becoming aware that something was required, he said shortly, "I am drinking a sherry. I don't suppose you want one, Miss Drover? And Marianne, what about you?"

On the point of refusing the sherry, Rosemary suddenly decided to put his lordship in his place. "Thank you, my lord," she said. "I would like a small glass, and I'm sure Marianne would enjoy a ratafia."

The Earl nodded to the butler, who disappeared.

"Dear Uncle Giles!" began Marianne. His lordship's eyebrows shot up to his dark wavy hair. "I mean, my lord," she amended, seeing his shock, "thank you for the lovely bedchamber."

As Rosemary bit her lip and looked down, trying not to laugh, Dear Uncle Giles responded carelessly, "Is it lovely? Don't thank me. I had nothing to do with it. It's all Mrs. Brown's doing. You may decide you want to use the furniture you brought with you. If so, address yourself to her."

When Marianne protested that she loved her new room as it was, he remarked, "It's all the same to me. I hardly ever go into the guest wing, except …"

He suddenly realized the rest of that sentence would reveal more than he wanted these two maidens to know, since the guest wing was where his lady visitors were invariably lodged, but luckily, Anstruther appeared at that moment with a tray. So he rapidly ended his sentence with "Very well. I will give orders for your own things to be stored until you need them."

Listening to this exchange, Rosemary was sure that was not what he had been going to say.

The butler handed a glass of ratafia to Marianne, and a second glass, which he filled with sherry, and gave to Miss Drover. Rosemary raised the delicate glass to her lips, knowing his lordship's eyes were upon her. She tasted the pale liquid and could barely restrain a shudder. It was sour and unpleasant, like some sort of cleaning fluid, she decided. Still, she was determined not to be beaten and took another small sip. She was ready for the taste this time, so she did not shudder, but it really was awful.

"You shouldn't ask for something you clearly do not like," said his lordship without a trace of humor in his voice. "It's a waste of good *fino*. Anstruther, take Miss Drover's glass away and bring her some ratafia."

Annoyed by his highhandedness, she protested, "I did not say I didn't like it. I have never had it before and thought I might try, that's all." Now she was annoyed with herself for responding like a scolded child.

Something of her displeasure must have made its way into her voice, for he lifted his mobile brow and responded, "You didn't have to say anything. Your face told the tale. But by all means, keep it. Leave it there, Anstruther."

Now she did not know what to do. She did not want the vile stuff, but neither did she want to give him the satisfaction of leaving it undrunk. She tried to change the subject while she unobtrusively (she thought) put down the small glass.

"My room is very pleasant, too, thank you," she said as brightly as she could. "It is very agreeable to have a fire in our rooms. We are not used to such luxury."

"Do you find it so? I'm afraid I find a fire in my room quite unremarkable. In this house you may expect no less, or the servants will hear about it."

"Oh, why is he determined to make everything I say sound idiotic," she thought, a little desperately. "He really is infuriating."

Then, Marianne, who had been sunk in contemplation of the logs on the fire, suddenly said artlessly, "What a comfortable room this is and how pleasant it is, sitting here! I feel entirely grown up! We never sat in the drawing room when Papa had guests. I suppose he thought us too young, well, me, at any rate, and he wouldn't have invited dear Rosie without me. Miss Drover, I mean."

"Indeed?" said Dear Uncle Giles repressively. "And Miss Drover has been your only governess?"

"Yes, she came when I was almost ten. She taught me everything: French, Geography, Drawing and Watercolors, Sewing, Good Manners, the Pianoforte … but she's much better at everything than I am. She's really clever, you know, especially at the piano!"

Rosemary protested and his lordship said, raising one eyebrow, "Then it is to be hoped, Marianne, that some of that has rubbed off on you. But you may play, Miss Drover, after dinner. We have an instrument here, you see." He did not wait for her to answer but waved at a shrouded shape at the end of the room and then said, unkindly, she thought, since he knew she did not like it, "Drink up your sherry, we are going into dinner. We sit down promptly at half past six."

So she was forced to drink down the rest of the liquid, which, in her opinion, might as well have been something to clear the drains. When she stood to leave the room, she suddenly felt quite dizzy. His lordship appeared not to notice, but led Marianne into the dining room. Anstruther offered Rosemary his arm, for which she was very grateful.

The long table that could seat at least thirty was set for just the three of them. Fortunately, although the Earl was, of course, at the head of the table, neither of the ladies present could count as hostess, so the other end remained empty. Instead, Rosemary and Marianne sat opposite each other in the middle. They were quite some way from his lordship, and not very close to one another either, as the table was wide. Moreover, there was a large silver epergne between them which quite blocked their view of each other. It was no doubt very fine workmanship, featuring a stag at bay, beneath an oak tree, surrounded by snarling dogs. However, it seemed inappropriate for the dinner table, and quite put Rosemary off her meal, until she contrived to ignore the images of death and dying. The epergne was full of apples and nuts, and she wondered if they were supposed to be eaten, or were only for decoration. The only way she and Marianne could see each other was to try to peep around the sides, which was fine if they both looked the same way at the same time. At first, they kept going in opposite directions, which occasioned stifled bursts of giggles from Marianne, until Rosemary hit upon the expedient of putting her napkin on the side she wished them to look around. Then they were able to carry on a muted communication, even if it was only by means of mouthed words and grimaces.

The meal was lengthy and formal, but at least it had the effect of quelling Rosemary's dizziness from the *fino*. The first course featured a paté of chicken and rabbit, turnips cooked in milk and butter, a monstrous ham, which his lordship, thankfully, carved for Anstruther to serve, and a dish of pickled cucumbers. There was a bottle of white wine, which Rosemary refused, thinking her foray into alcohol had been sufficient for the day. The second course was a haunch of venison, a mess of leeks, an apple pie and a huge piece of cheese. There was a red wine this time. Rosemary wondered how anyone could drink so much and yet appear perfectly normal. Finally, there was a lemon syllabub and a damson jelly, with yet more wine. Marianne had flagged after the ham and cucumbers, but perked up again when these sweets arrived.

Conversation was rather difficult, with the participants being so far separated. Rosemary asked about the epergne, which was, after all, very hard to ignore, but apart from telling her that his grandfather had brought it back from Bavaria and that it had always sat in the center of the table, his lordship had nothing more to say about it.

Finally, she plucked up her courage and said, "Do you think, my lord, that tomorrow Marianne and I could sit a place or two closer to you and without the epergne in front of us? You may have noticed we have been obliged to crane our necks to one side or the other to see each other."

"I did not notice anything," he responded, "but sit where you like. By all means, move up. Anstruther, see to it tomorrow."

"Thank you," Rosemary stood up. "Marianne, we will leave his lordship to his port."

Marianne, coming round to the door, turned, curtseyed deeply as if to royalty, and said, "It was a delicious dinner, thank you, Dear Uncle Giles."

Rosemary had to bite her lip and look down, as she tried not to smile at her charge's deliberate attempt both to make her wear the blue dress and to provoke the Earl. But all he said was, "Doing it up a bit too brown, Marianne, aren't you? But run along. I'll be in presently and Miss Drover shall play for us."

Rosemary nodded unwilling acquiescence and they both left the room. Once outside they had to smother their laughter as they went upstairs to wash their hands.

"*Dear Uncle Giles* and curtseying as if he were the Prince Regent!" Rosemary snorted. "Marianne, you are incorrigible!"

"I know, but he didn't say I mustn't call him that! So now you will have to wear that blue dress!" Marianne danced into her room. "Oh look, our things have arrived!"

Taking the time only to find her sheet music in her trunk, Rosemary did not look at herself in the mirror above the washstand in her room. She was not in the habit of looking at herself, since her mother had discouraged that form of pride, and anyway, her reflection was always uninspiring. If she had looked this evening, however, she would have seen a young woman whose curls now framed her face charmingly and, her color heightened by the warmth and the unaccustomed wine, a young woman whose face, while not exactly pretty, had an arresting quality, perhaps from the calm gaze of her wide eyes whose color seemed to change with the light. But as she urged her charge to stop rummaging in her trunk and come along, she did not see herself. Marianne took no notice but suddenly drew forth a very blue, short sleeved narrow gown, gathered into folds at the center of the shoulders in the back. It was in the new Empire style that Rosemary had copied from a *Mode Illustrée* lent by a neighbor, and she had been pleased with how well it had turned out. But Marianne was right. The color had never really suited her. She had only worn it once, at an afternoon tea ball given by the same neighbor whose daughter was due to be presented in London and who needed the dancing practice. Rosemary had played the piano, the young people had practiced their steps, and a fine time had been enjoyed by all.

Marianne was looking closely at the gown. "You know, Rosie, if you take out one of these gathers in the back, you will have enough material to lengthen the gown. And look!" She held the dress close to Rosemary's face. "It does make your eyes look blue! It really does!"

"Well, I'll think about it," conceded Rosemary. "But for now, let's put it aside and not keep Dear Uncle Giles waiting. Come along."

"But you said you'd dance a jig if we found you a blue dress, so come on! Dance!"

Rosemary laughed and, neatly executing a series of *pas de basque*, danced to the bedroom door, opened it and danced down the hall to the stairs. Then, as Marianne stifled her giggles, she stopped dancing and, her chin high and her mouth drawn into a solemn purse, proceeded in an exaggeratedly stately fashion down the stairs.

In the drawing room, his lordship was back in the armchair, staring vacantly into the fire.

"I'll never know what takes you ladies so long," he remarked. "You look exactly the same, so what have you been doing?"

"Our trunks arrived, Uncle Giles, and we were looking at our things. At least, I was," said Marianne still suppressing her giggles. "All Rosie did was to get out her sheet music." She was going to say *and dance a jig* but saw Rosemary's hasty shake of the head, so continued soberly, "I was persuading her to alter a blue dress she made for me so it will fit her. I think she'll look lovely in blue, don't you?"

"I'm no arbiter of women's fashions," said Uncle Giles, "but I imagine that just about anything would look better than the sackcloth she is presently wearing."

"That's what I said!" cried Marianne. "And I persuaded her to take off that awful cap. Don't you think she looks much better without it?"

"If you please, I would prefer your not discussing my person while I am standing here, or indeed, at any time," said Rosemary, speaking more calmly than she felt. So he *had* noticed her! And fancy calling her gown sackcloth! Then she changed the subject. "I shall go to the piano. Do you think it is in tune?"

"It had better be. I despise having things around me that are defective," said the Earl. "My servants all know that." He did not answer Marianne's question.

"And that had better warn you, my girl," thought Rosemary. "You had better not be defective in your playing, or the servants will toss you out." She smiled, but since her back was by now to the others, no one saw it.

She walked around the pianoforte, sat down, lifted the lid, adjusted the seat to her height and began to play Mozart's *Turkish March*. She had brought the music, but, in truth, did not need it as she had been playing the piece for years. It amazed her that Mozart had composed this piece when he was not much older than she was now. It was the last movement of his 11th Sonata for piano and was basically a round, with the theme being repeated in various ways, but she marveled at how he had taken such a simple idea and made it transcendent.

Her touch was deft and light as she began and, as always when playing, she lost herself. When the Earl looked at her, he could hardly believe this was the same nondescript woman he had travelled with that morning. She was lightly tossing her head in tempo with the music, her eyes, were they blue? brown? grey? sparkling, a half smile on her lips. As the piece came to its final, almost military, conclusion, she at last appeared to come back into herself and looked down, striking the keys with verve and passion. It was a performance all the more remarkable for being completely unexpected.

Marianne clapped her hands. "Oh, I love it when you play that piece. It always makes me happy!"

"Yes, me too," said Rosemary, rising from the piano. "I can almost see the Turkish band and feel the sun on my shoulders."

"You played it well," was his lordship's more sedate response. "Will you not play again?"

Rosemary sat down again and, after a little thought, played the slow, melodic first movement of Beethoven's *Moonlight Sonata*. It was a complete change from the Mozart, with its almost somber, elegiac mood. When the last notes had died softly away, there was a moment of complete silence before Marianne said, "I don't know why Beethoven found the moonlight so sad! I always think it should be happy – lovers meeting in the moonlight and that sort of thing," she blushed and glanced quickly at her uncle, "but he must have had another idea entirely!"

"I congratulate you on your knowledge of the composer, Marianne, for which no doubt Miss Drover is responsible, but I would be interested to know whence comes your idea of lovers in the moonlight. It must be the result of your reading material. I'm surprised, Miss Drover, that you encourage such rubbish."

"Oh, Rosie doesn't encourage it, Uncle Giles," came the quick retort. "It's just that I like novels so much more than all those dreary French philosophers she's always trying to get me to read. Suffering for one's love is always a feature of those stories, it seems."

Rosemary saw his lordship's eyebrows rise, but before he could say anything, she broke in, "Perhaps Beethoven was acquainted with lovers who had an uncle who felt as you do, my lord. That would explain the tone of the piece."

The Earl made as if to retort, but then simply said, "Touché, Miss Drover!" Decidedly, he thought, this governess-companion was a most unusual person. To look at her, one would dismiss her as a complete nonentity, but she clearly had hidden depths.

But the person in question had risen and closed the lid of the piano. "If you will permit, my lord," she said, uncomfortably aware that her unguarded comment had been too much a criticism of their host and feeling wrong-footed once again, "we will go up now. I know I'm very tired and I'm sure Marianne is too."

"By all means," came the neutral response, "and thank you for playing. It was ... illuminating."

He rose and went to open the door for them. Marianne gave him another pretty curtsey, but Rosemary merely bowed and muttered, "Good night, my lord. I hope you sleep well." She was hanged if she would curtsey to him!

When they returned to their bedchambers, they found that their luggage had been unpacked and their things put away. Marianne was ecstatic: she had never had a maid do that for her before and considered it the height of luxury. Rosemary was more circumspect. She knew from her mother's advice that if one were staying somewhere where one's clothing was unpacked for one, one had better make sure to have the best quality underclothing possible. No one was more critical of old and dingy linen than the maids and dressers in country homes, and no one quicker to judge the social standing of the owners of such items. What message her meagre assortment of darned and patched things must have sent, she could only well imagine.

While living at Fairchild Court, she had, of course, received a salary, but it had not been generous, and she had preferred spending her money on books and music. It did not matter if her underwear, or outerwear, come to that, were darned and patched. Here, things would undoubtedly be different. That led her to another thought. What exactly was her situation here? Would she continue to receive the salary of a governess, small as it was, or, as a *companion,* would her board and lodging be considered sufficient remuneration? As much as she hated to do so, she would have to speak to the Earl. She sighed and prepared for bed with that unwelcome interview in mind.

As usual, before going to bed herself, she went in to see Marianne. That young lady was sitting up in her bed, her hair braided, wearing a very becoming night cap and looking pleased with herself.

"You know, Rosie," she said, "I think we shall be very comfortable here. To be sure, I miss my old home, but it would have been impossible to stay there with *that woman*, even if she had wanted us." She shuddered. "She never gave us a fire in our rooms, nor had the maids put a hot brick in the bed. Ooh!" she exclaimed, sitting up straighter, "do you think they'll bring us tea in the morning? Now *that* would be a luxury!"

"We'll just have to wait and see," replied Rosemary, plumping up her pillows and encouraging her to lie down. "Try to sleep now, love, instead of contemplating what treats may be in store. You must be tired. I know I am!" She made to leave.

"Wait a minute, Rosie! I took that blue dress out for you. The maids had hung it up. Take it away and alter it for yourself! You promised, you know you did!"

Shaking her head with a rueful smile, Rosemary picked up the gown and went back to her room.

Chapter Five

Marianne's dream of luxury came true the next morning when a maid brought tea at eight o'clock, built up the fire and asked if she would like to breakfast in her room. Marianne gleefully said yes, but Rosemary, deciding unwillingly that she had better get her interview with the Earl over as soon as possible, asked what his lordship's morning habits were. She was told that the Earl generally rode for an hour in the mornings before having a late breakfast. She therefore drank her tea slowly, considering what she might say to him. Then she dressed in her usual uncompromising fashion, pulling her cap over her forehead and covering all her tightly braided hair.

She entered the dining room to discover his lordship reading the newspaper and drinking coffee. He did not look up as she came in, and continued to read the paper while she stood in silence. Her limited experience of gentlemen had taught her that they were often grouchy in the mornings and did not like to be disturbed.

"Yes? What is it?" he said finally, still without looking up.

"I'm sorry to disturb you, my lord," she began, but before she could say another word, he looked up, and seeing who it was, rose with a sigh from his seat.

"Miss Drover!" he said, not sounding pleased to see her. "I thought it was Anstruther creeping about. Why are you standing there like that?"

"You looked engrossed and…"

"Well, for God's sake sit down."

Rosemary hesitated and finally sat at a place half way between where she had been the night before and the Earl's place at the head of the table. The epergne glowered dully in the center of the table, and Rosemary turned resolutely from it. "My lord," she began, but then the door opened and Anstruther came in.

"Miss Drover," he pronounced. "I only just learned you have come down for breakfast. If I had known to expect you, I would have brought you coffee, unless you prefer tea?"

"I'm sorry, Anstruther," she began again. Really, she thought, was she going to spend the whole morning apologizing? "I didn't think of it until I was in bed last night. I need to speak to his lordship and I thought…"

"Just tell him whether you want tea or coffee," interrupted the Earl. "He doesn't need the whole story."

"Coffee, please, Anstruther," she said obediently and, as the butler left the room, began again. "My lord, as I said, I'm sorry to disturb you but…"

"Yes, yes, no need to rehearse all that. Just tell me what you want."

Rosemary drew in a deep breath. "I would like to know exactly what… what my situation is here. As you know, I was Marianne's governess and for that I received a salary. Now that I am a… a companion, I wonder…"

"What did the old skinflint pay you?" interrupted his lordship. "Not much, I'll be bound. I don't suppose he thought the education of females worth much. Nor do I, come to that."

Rosemary was so incensed by this casual remark that before she could prevent herself, she burst out, "The education of females not worth much? And who do you think, my lord, are the first educators of all children, male and female? Mothers, nurses and nannies. All women. And how are they to educate the future leaders of our country if they are ignorant themselves? Would you want the heir to your position brought up by women who know nothing?" She was on the point of saying, "Is that how you were brought up yourself, which from your lack of manners I judge to be so?" but stopped herself just in time. Instead, she said, "My mother, the wisest and best woman I have ever known or expect to know, told me that an educated mother means an educated family. I daresay you will tell me that Eton and Harrow are responsible for our young men's minds, but let me tell you, my lord, that unless those minds have been prepared by the women in the home and nursery, they will never reach their true fulfillment."

The Earl looked at her in amazement. He was entirely unused to being lectured in this way. No one in the household would dare to do so, and that this pitiful governess should dare to take issue with his opinion took him completely off guard. Speech forsook him and for several moments there was complete silence in the dining room. It was fortunate that Anstruther chose that moment to come in with a cup and a pot of coffee.

He appeared not to notice the fraught atmosphere, but placed the cup in front of Rosemary and filled it, saying, "You will find breakfast foods laid out on the side table, Miss Drover. May I bring you toast?"

"No, thank you, Anstruther," she replied, acutely uncomfortable, and wishing she could just disappear. "I shall not be eating."

The butler refilled the Earl's cup, placed the coffee pot on the table, bowed and left. Rosemary sipped her coffee mechanically, wondering what she should say or do. Finally, lifting her head and looking at his lordship, she said, "I must apologize, my lord. I had no right to lecture you at your own table. My mother also used to tell me I was too outspoken and urged me to curb my tongue. It's a pity I didn't learn that lesson as well as I learned the one I repeated to you." She fell silent for a moment, but when no response came from the end of the table, she continued, "If you have no place for me at High House, I shall understand."

The coffee-pouring hiatus had given the Earl time to recover from his angry amazement and in spite of himself, he was struck by Rosemary's words. He found himself thinking of his own mother. He remembered the songs she had sung to help him sleep when he was disturbed as a child, and the times she had calmed him down with her gentle explanations from the tantrums he often experienced when disappointed or crossed. She had died when he was in his early teens and at Eton. He had mourned her but, already feeling himself a man, had pushed those memories to the back of his mind. After her death, there was no one to explain when he was wrong, or help him deal with disappointment without lashing out. His intemperate nature met little check, and by the time of his father's death and his accession to the title some ten years later, no one dared to gainsay a man known for his uncertain temper.

But he knew there was truth in what the governess had said. The best of his nature was what his mother had taught him. As a man at the head of an important estate surrounded by people who bowed to his will, if he was now able to reason with himself and act with something like moderation even when angry, it was because of the lessons she had inculcated in him. Therefore, when Rosemary apologized and offered to leave, as much as he would have liked to tell her to go to the devil, he did not.

"Don't be ridiculous, Miss Drover," he said, shortly. "Though we may disagree on the value of education for women, we need you at High House. Marianne needs a chaperone, for one thing. And there may be something in what you say, although what type of lessons Marianne will be able to teach her children when her head seems full of romantic nonsense, it is hard to imagine."

It was on the tip of Rosemary's tongue to contradict his lordship again, and she opened her mouth to speak, but he continued, "However, I am reasonably sure that is not what you wanted to talk to me about, so cut line and out with it."

Thus commanded, Rosemary took a deep breath and without preamble said, "I wanted to know if I am still to receive a governess's salary, even though I am, apparently, no longer a governess." There, she thought, that's giving it to him plainly. "And you asked me just now what salary I received. I was paid five pounds a quarter."

"Just as I thought! The old skinflint got you for nothing. Good God, I pay my housemaids more than that. But you probably didn't know any better. Why did you become a governess, Miss Drover? I have the impression you were not raised in that expectation."

As briefly and unemotionally as she could, Rosemary told him about the death of her parents and the need for her to find employment. She spoke softly, looking down at her hands, and he again had the impression that she was younger than he had imagined.

"Tell me, Miss Drover," he said abruptly, "what is your age?"

Rosemary looked up at him, fixing her unusual wide eyes on his face. "I'm twenty-three," she said, fully expecting that this was the end. She was no longer needed as a governess and she was too young to be a chaperone.

His lordship looked at her, seeing the welter of emotions passing in her eyes. She was fearful but her gaze was steady. Then he remembered the head tossing, passionate piano player of the previous evening and saw her in the sad, drab person before him. It no longer seemed amazing that she should be so outspoken. Here was a woman of education and opinions, forced into a situation of servitude. He suddenly felt sorry for her.

"Well, I rely on you to relieve Marianne of the tripe that seems to occupy her mind at the moment. She seems to have pretty enough manners, and if she can only develop some sort of sensible conversation I daresay she will pass off quite well when she is introduced into London society. I shall double your salary."

It was Rosemary's turn to sit in amazement. She had expected to be dismissed, but instead, her salary was to be increased. Doubled! "Th... thank you, my lord," she stammered.

"Don't thank me. I'm not paying it." replied the Earl, dismissively. "Marianne's fortune is quite sufficient to support her own staff. But for God's sake, use some of it to buy yourself a new wardrobe. You will be in Marianne's company around the neighborhood and you cannot go looking like a refugee from the workhouse. Talk to Mrs. Brown, the housekeeper. There's some sort of woman who comes around to do the sewing, I believe. That is all. You may go." He turned back to his newspaper.

Rosemary got to her feet in a daze. She walked to the door, turned, and before she could prevent herself, curtseyed. "Good morning, my lord," she said, and quietly left. But, his eyes on the pages in front of him, he did not notice this most unusual courtesy on the part of Miss Drover.

When she got back upstairs, Marianne had left her bed and was sitting on the window bench, peering out of the casement, still dressed in her nightgown.

"Oh look, Rosie!" she said, in her usual exuberant manner, "There's a ruin in the grounds, over there! All in the mists! How romantic! We must walk over there. Do you think there are ghosts at night? I must say, I didn't hear any wailing or clanking of chains. I slept like a log! But just think, how deliciously frightening if there were! Let's stay awake tonight and keep watch."

Rosemary looked out the window, and sure enough, below them in the near distance, on the descending slope of the hill that gave High House its name, there was what looked to be a ruin of a church. The roofless bell tower was clear enough in the morning sunshine, but on the slope below it, a mist still swirled as the earth warmed up from the overnight chill, so that it seemed to rise magically from a cloud. It was indeed a romantic vision and normally she would have joined Marianne in imagining all sorts of stories, but this morning, after her interview with the Earl, she felt obliged to depress the notion.

"Don't be silly," she said repressively. "We can walk down there, by all means, but I expect it's just a falling-down old church left from the time of Cromwell. The only wailing you're likely to hear is your own, when a stone falls on your head! Anyway, come away from the window. Anyone walking by might see you in your nightgown."

Marianne turned to look at her, disappointed at not being supported in her imaginative illusions. "Oh, Rosie! Don't be such a stick-in-the-mud! And why are you wearing that horrid old cap again? Take it off! It makes you look about ninety years old!"

"Very well," replied her governess, or chaperone, or companion, whatever she was, untying the ribbons of her headwear, "Since it appears you are actually my employer, I must do as you say. You are doubling my salary, by the way. Thank you, Madam," and she bobbed a curtsey.

Marianne gave a peal of laughter. "Am I? Who says so? How funny!"

"His lordship has informed me that your fortune is ample enough to support your staff, which is me, and with my new-found riches I am to dress myself appropriately, so that I am fit to be seen by the neighbors."

"*Dear* Uncle Giles! He is quite right. You know, I think he may not be so bad, after all. I am getting to quite like him!"

"You won't like him so much when he says your head is full of tripe and I have to teach you to make sensible conversation."

"You're making that up!" protested Marianne.

Thinking she should not have been so frank in relaying his lordship's comments, Rosemary answered, "Perhaps I am. At any rate, it's true that you should be able to converse sensibly on a range of innocent topics. Nothing too clever! We women have to walk a fine line between appearing too knowledgeable and empty-headed. Anyway, we will stop making up stories and instead talk about ... well, about the latest play on in London, what is happening at Court, or, since we know nothing about either of those things, the weather, I suppose."

"*The weather*? What on earth is there to say about that?"

"Well, one can always begin: 'it's very warm/cold/rainy/foggy for the time of the year, don't you think?' And then listen to the answer and take a cue from there. The most important thing is to make the gentleman think that everything he says is the most interesting thing you ever heard. It can work as well for any matrons you may want to impress, but generally speaking, women are more likely to recognize fudge when they hear it. Let us practice. I'll be the gentleman. You begin."

Marianne sat on the edge of the bed and said demurely, "It has been particularly foggy for the time of the year, don't you think, Uncle Giles?"

"No more than usual, I think. What makes you say that?"

"Rosie!" protested the younger woman, "You aren't supposed to ask me a question to answer a question!"

"No, but it's a good technique. Anyway, carry on."

"Oh, er… well, Uncle Giles, when I looked out of my window this morning, I could see mist swirling around the ruins."

"That is because the atmosphere was warmer than the ground. It burns off quite quickly. That's normal for this time of the year."

"Really? How interesting! Um… would you say it is more common here in Kent than elsewhere?"

"I doubt it."

Marianne waited for Rosemary to carry on, and when she did not, protested again, "But Rosie! You have to help!"

"Since I'm supposed to be Dear Uncle Giles, I'm reacting the way he would. I doubt if he would help the conversation at all. If you can converse with him, you can converse with anyone! Carry on!"

"Dear Uncle Giles, you know so much about everything, I could talk to you for hours!" Marianne suffocated a giggle.

"Don't be ridiculous, Marianne! I'm surprised Miss Drover has taught you to utter such obvious falsehoods."

Marianne gasped. "He wouldn't say that!"

"Oh, yes he would, and I wouldn't blame him. You must try to make your flattery more subtle. Of course, there are many gentlemen who are so convinced of their own superiority that no flattery may be too extreme. But, somehow, I don't think Dear Uncle Giles falls into that category. Anyway, time to get dressed." Rosemary looked out the window. "Look, it is just as he said, the mist is burning off. Put on your boots and we'll have a tramp over there."

"Silly! He didn't say it – you did! Oh, dear Miss Drover! You know so much about everything! I could talk to you for hours!"

And they both burst out laughing.

Chapter Six

Donning their cloaks and boots, the two ladies set out across the lawn to the ruined church. Their rooms overlooked the back of the house, and as she turned to look at it, Rosemary could see it was shaped like an E without the center line. It was of a light honey-colored stone, which she later came to know was the limestone indigenous to the high Weald. Along the long line of the E, the gabled second floor windows together with a crenellated roof line, gave the house a pleasantly antique appearance, though she thought it could not be older than seventeenth century. It was two stories high, but because it was built on a slope, what was the cellar floor had half-windows at the back. The unusual feature was a round tower at the end of each wing. These looked almost like salt and pepper pots, with plain stone walls surmounted by a series of gabled openings all around the top. It was as if a giant could pick them up and shake them upside down to flavor his food.

Rosemary pointed this out to Marianne, who laughed and said, "Who's being fanciful now? If you can have your salt and pepper pots, I can have my ghost!"

By now the mist had cleared and as they came down the slope to where the ruins stood, the church looked much bigger than it had from their bedroom windows. The bell tower rose above them as they went through the space where the doors must have once stood. Inside, the stone supports remained mostly intact but it was obvious that anything made of wood had long since disappeared. The stone arches of the nave and the chancel were still there, but the roof they were built to support was open to the sky.

"All the wood must have burned at some point," mused Rosemary. "Probably Cromwell's army, though it could have been an accident, I suppose. I wonder why they didn't use the stone to build the house – it's much later than the church. Someone must have decided to leave it alone. Perhaps the first Earl. Let's ask Dear Uncle Giles tonight at dinner. In fact, you bring it up, Marianne, so he'll know you have some intelligent conversation."

"I think it's wonderful!" said Marianne, twirling around in the empty nave. "But it really isn't scary at all, now we're down here. It's lovely in the sunlight! It would be a wonderful place for a picnic – or, I know! An open-air play. You could write one and we could perform it here. The actors could appear from behind the pillars and act out the story in the nave! It would be perfect! Do you think Uncle Giles would let us?"

"I don't think the problem would be Uncle Giles' permission so much as the idea of *actors.* Where would they come from? There's only the two of us! Or perhaps you're thinking he might take part. If that's part of your plan, I advise you to give it up right away!"

"Oh Rosie! Don't be such a killjoy! There must be other people in the neighborhood! Why, even back at home there were the Makepeaces and the Killingtons, and old Mrs. Townsend, though I can't imagine her being in a play! She must be ninety if she's a day! But Mrs. Killington would have let Sarah act in anything you wrote. She had a very high opinion of you. When you played for Sarah's day ball, I heard her saying to Mrs. Makepeace that she had never met anyone as clever and cultured as you and how lucky my father was to have found you!"

"Well, I'll think about it. Perhaps in a few months when we've made the acquaintance of our neighbors, if there are any. Let's go back up to the house and walk around it. It really is quite large and I find the architecture interesting."

Marianne looked at her but gave no response. She could not understand her companion's desire to look at buildings. At home in the library there had been a book by a man with the odd name of Batty Langley that Rosemary had encouraged her to study. She had quite liked his illustrations of arched and pointed windows; they seemed romantic. But that was as far as it went. When it came to comparing the pictures of Mr. Langley's pillars with those in another book that were apparently Greek, Marianne thought it was going too far. Rosemary had called them *columns* and said that Mr. Langley's style was called Gothick and the other book was Palladian, but in Marianne's opinion a pillar was a pillar and that was an end to it. She sighed and prepared herself for a lecture on the architecture of High House.

But she was saved the lecture, for when they had walked back up the hill, passing the stables set off on their right and around one of the pepper pot towers to the front of the house, they encountered the Earl. He had evidently been talking to a man who, touching his whip to his hat, rode off just as they arrived.

"Uncle Giles!" cried Marianne, running up to him. "We were in the ruined chapel just now and it's the perfect place for an open-air play. Rosemary's going to write one specially. You won't object, will you?" Seeing Rosemary frown, she collected herself, bobbed a curtsey and said quickly, "And good morning, by the way."

His lordship looked somewhat stunned at Marianne's unconventional greeting and Rosemary hurried to intervene.

"Marianne! How can you rattle on so to his lordship? I'm sure he has no notion what you're talking about. And you know the question of a play in the chapel is by no means settled! It was just an idea!" And turning to the Earl "I'm sorry, my lord, but Marianne is inclined to be over-enthusiastic when something has caught her fancy."

"I collect that what has caught her fancy, as you put it," said his lordship, "is some sort performance in the ruins at the bottom of the hill. As for my approval, I would have to know details before I could say one way or the other."

He began to walk towards the front door, but then turned. "Before I forget, I received a note this morning from our nearest neighbor, Mrs. Hardcastle, begging leave to call on you as soon as may be convenient with her son and daughter, I can't remember their names. I imagine they have heard of your arrival through the servants; I certainly haven't broadcast it. Here," he reached into his pocket, "I shall pass you the note, Miss Drover, and you may reply as you see fit. I would, however, prefer that you delay any social engagement until you can appear more appropriately dressed than at present. I cannot have the neighbors imagining that I have employed a person from the workhouse as companion for my ward. Please do whatever is necessary to improve your wardrobe. I'm sure Mrs. Brown can advise you. Have the bills sent to me."

And with that, he went into the house and left them open-mouthed on the parterre.

Marianne was the first to recover, as she had stopped listening after the mention of a neighbor who had both a son and a daughter.

"There! What did I say, Rosie! There *are* neighbors! And they want to meet us!" She skipped a little jig.

Miss Drover was still smarting from the Earl's last remarks. She did not know whether to be gratified that he required her to buy a new wardrobe and send him the bills, or insulted by the reference to herself as looking like the inmate of the workhouse. She had never been particularly interested in her appearance, apart from wanting to be neat and tidy, but it had not occurred to her that anyone would find her so unpleasant to look at. She determined there and then to show him! The workhouse, indeed!

"Then I must hurry up and refurbish that blue dress, I suppose," she said. "That will be the quickest way forward if I'm not to be seen in public dressed as I am. Anyway, let's finish our tour of the outside of the house." She walked on, still pondering his lordship's remarks.

Marianne followed her along the front of the building with its tall windows, plain on the ground floor but gable-topped on the upper story. They went around the "pepper pot" turret at the end, which also featured gabled windows all around the top. Luckily for Marianne, her companion was so sunk in her own thoughts that she did not, as she usually did, give a running commentary on the architecture of what they were looking at. In fact, though the whole place had a medieval air, Rosemary had already decided it was of a much later date and had determined to ask the Earl at luncheon. They saw that the kitchen garden and greenhouses were off to the right, and as they rounded that wing they could smell the aroma of what was probably luncheon emanating from the kitchens. Rosemary realized she was quite hungry. She had eaten no breakfast during her fraught interview with his lordship.

"Mmm! That smells nice!" commented Marianne, who still had the hearty appetite of late girlhood. "Come on Rosie, I'm *starving*!"

They entered the house at the back, where they had come out, and made their way quickly up two flights of stairs to their bedchambers. The beds had been made, the rooms swept and tidied and there was warm water in the washstand ewers.

"This is nuts for us!" cried Marianne from her room into Rosemary's, "*warm* water – what a treat!" She enthusiastically washed her hands. "And I *love* this rose soap. I tell you, Rosie, I like it here!"

"Then you'd better not let his lordship hear you using such vulgar expressions as *nuts for us*. I have the impression he is quite a stickler and he'll send you off to some sort of finishing school. I don't even know where you learned such a thing."

"Oh, it's what Bertie Makepeace used to say all the time. Don't worry. I'll be all *prunes, prisms and papa* for Dear Uncle Giles!"

Rosemary could not help laughing as she urged her charge out of the room and down the stairs, so for the second time, Anstruther, carrying a salver with a bottle of Médoc into the dining room for his lordship, heard them and smiled.

The Earl rose from his seat looking rather surprised as they entered, as if he had forgotten their existence, but said nothing. Their places had been moved closer to the head of the table and they were now able to see each other clearly without the impediment of the epergne. The luncheon was only somewhat lighter than the dinner of the night before. There was almost as much formality and as many dishes. Rosemary wondered if they were to eat like this every day and hoped not: she thought she would soon need a whole new wardrobe just to fit her waist, never mind pleasing his lordship. However, she ate with good appetite and once her hunger was assuaged, was on the point of asking his lordship the origins of High House when Marianne said brightly, "Uncle Giles! The ruined chapel was quite swathed in mist this morning. Just the bell tower rose into the sunlight. Is that usual for this time of the year?"

Uncle Giles, just bringing a forkful of beef to his mouth, stopped his hand in midair and replied in surprise, "Of course it is! I'm surprised you haven't learned that such mist occurs when the ground is colder than the air above it. It tends to happen in the spring and autumn. The warmth of the sun causes it to disappear quite quickly, as I'm sure you saw this morning."

"That is *so* interesting, Uncle Giles! Now you explain it, I do remember Rosie... er, Miss Drover, telling me something about it before. But it is so startling to see when you're on a hill looking down. We didn't have anything like that at Fairchild Court. I wonder if we shall find other weather phenomena different from at home."

The Earl, chewing his mouthful of food, made no reply to this, but Rosemary, silently congratulating her pupil on masterfully managing to flatter her uncle and respond to an implied criticism of herself while talking of nothing but the weather, gave her a warm smile and said, "I'm sure as the days go on we will find many things different here in the High Weald of Kent." Then, turning to their beleaguered host who had just started to raise his fork once more, asked, "My lord, is there perhaps a book in the library here that outlines the origins of High House? I find its architecture so interesting."

The Earl sighed and put down his fork. "It was built by the first Earl in the early seventeen hundreds, though, as you have no doubt noticed, he favored an earlier style. He was influenced by Craigcrook Castle in Scotland, which he had had occasion to visit and was much impressed by. That is a good deal older, of course.

He decided he would have two round towers instead of one, as they have there. He also decided to keep the ruined chapel as it is. He liked its antiquity. He did keep all the drawings and plans, which are indeed in the library. Now, if you will excuse me, I should like to finish my luncheon in peace. I have much to attend to this afternoon and do not have time for idle chatter." He picked up his fork.

"Of course, my lord," muttered Rosemary, looking down at her plate.

She heard what sounded like a stifled giggle from Marianne and, looking up at her through her lashes, saw that maiden rolling her eyes and surreptitiously putting an upright finger across her lips in the universal signal for quiet. She had difficulty swallowing a smile. His lordship, chewing a mouthful of his lunch, saw the look that passed between the two women and the humor that played around the edges of Rosemary's lips, and felt that he had somehow become an object of amusement to the two women. It was not a feeling he was at all accustomed to.

The luncheon came to an end with little more being said. The ladies rose. Marianne curtseyed with a "Thank you for a delicious luncheon, Uncle Giles". Rosemary inclined her head as he rose from his seat, and they left him, looking, it must be said, quite relieved at their departure.

Free of restraint, Marianne giggled all the way upstairs, in spite of her companion's urgent entreaty to hush.

"I talked about the weather, you talked about architecture and *still* he wasn't even remotely amused," she exclaimed. "That's it! My goal from now on is to make Dear Uncle Giles laugh. Really laugh! I don't think he's had any fun in *years*."

"It's more likely that we'll end up taking our meals in the nursery," replied Rosemary, prosaically. "It's probably best to let him eat in silence. It seems to be what he prefers. Now, to bring your mind into more appropriate channels, I think you should practice your French for an hour or so by writing out seven of Pascal's *Pensées* and translating them. I shall work on that blue dress."

In spite of Marianne's huffing and puffing, that is exactly what they did. Marianne sat at her desk, at first spending more time mending her pen and then chewing the end of it, before becoming quite engrossed in her work. Rosemary unpicked the gathered back of the blue gown and found that there was indeed enough material for her to cut out two of the folds to lengthen it. She carefully cut the piece out and pinned the rest back. It still fell in sufficient gathers to look more or less as it should. Luckily, although she was quite tall, her figure was slim and the fabric still floated over her derrière. Gathering up the pieces, she took them downstairs to the ironing room for pressing.

While there, she ran into Mrs. Brown, the housekeeper, and ascertained that Mrs. Croft, the seamstress, would be there in two days. Once she explained his lordship's requirement for her to have new gowns, Mrs. Brown entered into the affair with enthusiasm.

"If you have images of the gowns you need, provided they are not too complicated I'm sure Mrs. Croft would be delighted to make them up," she said excitedly. "She would no doubt welcome the change from repairing sheets and tablecloths and monogramming the handkerchiefs."

"I can assure you, they are not complicated," Rosemary replied with a laugh. "I have been making Miss Marianne's dresses for some time now, and although I pride myself that the results are not to be despised, I certainly cannot do anything very unusual!"

"Then between you, I'm sure you and Mrs. Croft will achieve very creditable results. We can use material from her ladyship's gowns stored in the attics. Come and see. You will have to ask his lordship, of course, but since you are following his instructions, I'm sure he will not object. I have always found him a most reasonable man, and I think most of the staff would say the same."

Rosemary was somewhat surprised at this encomium of the Earl from his housekeeper, but said nothing. They went up to the attics and there, in old trunks, carefully folded in silk paper interleaved with lavender, were beautiful gowns in sumptuous fabrics; out of date gowns with rigid bodices and voluminous skirts that would have been worn over hoops and panniers. Marianne held them up to herself and waltzed around while Rosemary ran her fingers over the treasure trove, finally deciding on a shining amber silk, a violet lustring with a beaded hem and a dark blue velvet. While most of the fabrics were stiff bombazines or heavy with embroidery, beads, and trim, these were supple enough to adapt to the current mode of gowns fitted under the bosom and falling almost straight to the feet in front, with soft folds in the back.

"Look at this black velvet cloak," exclaimed Mrs. Brown. "The lining is in poor condition but I'm sure Mrs. Croft could furbish it up. If I may say, Miss Drover, your own cloak is in dire need of replacement. Let's see what can be done."

Rosemary went back to her own room, more excited at the prospect of a new wardrobe than she would have thought possible for a woman who, up till then, had given her clothing very little consideration.

For the rest of the afternoon she worked on the alterations to the blue gown, while listening to Marianne first read the French, then her translation. While the younger woman was far from being bookish, she could acquit herself quite well when she put her mind to it. Thus the afternoon passed very pleasantly. At one point, Mrs. Brown, who had been told of Miss Drover's intention to lengthen the blue dress, came in with a piece of navy-blue braid which had been left over from a long-ago nanny's gown. When sewn around the seam where the strip had been added to the bottom of the dress, the addition looked intentional. By dinner time, it was ready.

When Rosemary put it on, she was transformed. In place of the shapeless round gown that fit her nowhere, the slim blue dress allowed her figure to appear, highlighting her shapely bosom and narrow waist. The only jewelry she possessed, besides the locket with her grandparents' hair, were her mother's wedding ring and pearls. As wife of a rector, that lady had worn very little ornamentation. So she put her mother's pearls around her creamy throat and brushed her chestnut curls onto the top of her head, where she anchored them with some of Marianne's pins. She was completely unrecognizable as the dowdy governess who had left Fairfield Court.

Marianne danced around her companion. "I *told* you that color would become you! I was quite right! Your eyes look very blue and your hair is really pretty done like that."

"You look very nice yourself in that pink muslin," replied Rosemary. "How lucky we were Mrs. Killington decided it didn't suit Sarah. She was quite right, of course. With her reddish gold curls it would not have done at all."

"Won't Uncle Giles be surprised to have two pretty ladies at his dinner table," laughed Marianne as they went towards the stairs. "Perhaps he'll even smile!"

"But remember what you just translated from Pascal," smiled Rosemary. *"We love a person only on account of borrowed qualities."*

"Oh Rosie! Trust you to say that!"

Chapter Seven

At six on the dot the two women entered the drawing room to find it empty, so the grand effect at least one of them was hoping to produce was lost. Marianne slumped unceremoniously into the settle and said, "Well! When he warned us yesterday to be punctual!" She imitated the Earl in a pompous voice: *"We sit down promptly at half past six."*

"And so we do," came a voice from the doorway. "This evening is no different, though I am a little late home. I told you I was very busy this afternoon. Ask Anstruther for whatever you wish. I shall change and be back directly." And his lordship strode swiftly off in the direction of the stairs.

"He didn't even look at you!" exclaimed Marianne, not a whit disconcerted at being overheard. "What a beast!"

"Hush, Marianne!" said Rosemary. "It was good of him to bother to tell us he was late. This is his home, after all! He can come and go as he pleases! Now sit up properly and have a little more decorum. It can serve no good purpose to be rude to your uncle."

Indeed, the Earl had not noticed Miss Drover, as he had only stood in the doorway and she had been bent over the piano stool at the other end of the room, arranging her music, but as he left he heard Marianne's remark and her reply and wondered what he should have observed.

When he returned, barely fifteen minutes later, he saw. His reaction to her transformation was perhaps not as effusive as Marianne would have liked, but for a man of the Earl's careful disposition, hard learned after a youth of indiscretion, it was unusually warm. When he came in, she was standing with her back to the fire looking at one of the bibelots that sat on a side table. Her hair shone richly and the light behind her outlined her shape. He saw for the first time that, while she was very slim, she had a good figure. The shadows accentuated the hills of her bosom and the pearls glowed against her white throat.

"I may be a beast," he glanced at Marianne, who had the grace to blush, "but allow me to congratulate you, Miss Drover," he said, stopping a few feet from her and appraising her frankly from head to toe. "I would not have recognized you. I think we may safely say the workhouse is behind us. How came you to obtain a gown so quickly?"

"It was one of mine, Uncle Giles," said Marianne quickly. "Rosie made it for me a little while ago but the color never became me. She altered it for herself this afternoon. It was too short, so she unpicked the back and ..."

"His lordship doesn't want to know all the details, my love," interrupted Rosemary, who had felt her color rising at the scrutiny she had just been subjected to and desired nothing more than to end this conversation. "Suffice it to say, I was able to modify it to fit myself."

His lordship went to pick up the glass of *fino* Anstruther had left for him. Rosemary hesitated, "I do not want to persist in a discussion which must, I feel, be of very little interest to you, but since we are on the subject, may I ask you, my lord, if I may adapt some of her late ladyship's gowns for my use. They are in a trunk in the attic. It would be the quickest way for me to improve my wardrobe as you have directed."

"Is there no end to your accomplishments, Miss Drover?" replied the Earl with more humor in his voice than either of the women had hitherto heard. He waved her to a chair, before sitting down himself. "I imagine that would involve more than simply ... er *unpicking*. But you may certainly use anything in the attics. Even if my mother were still alive, I doubt she would remember them. She was wont to change her garments with a frequency that would astonish you."

"Oh, Rosie is really good at dressmaking!" chimed in Marianne. "She makes all my things. She made this." She stood up and twirled around in her pink muslin.

"Very pretty. But I think you should employ a dressmaker in future. Miss Drover has enough to do without making your clothes. Your father seems to have left a great deal to her offices. You must ask Mrs. Hardcastle whom she uses."

"I don't mind doing it, my lord," said Rosemary quickly. I find it quite soothing."

"And she makes me read and translate French while she sews!" added Marianne, anxious to convince her guardian that she, too had been usefully occupied.

"Indeed! And is that what you did this afternoon?" In spite of himself, the Earl was intrigued. His only exposure to how women spent their time had been from his mother and the various *chères amies* he had had under his protection, and they typically went shopping or visited friends for an afternoon of gossip.

"Yes," responded Marianne, before Rosemary could answer. "And we spent a long time discussing Pascal's idea that we never really love a person for themselves, but for their qualities, even though these might change. For example, if you love a woman for her beauty, but she gets smallpox and her beauty is ruined, can you still love her? What do you think, Uncle Giles? Do you think you can distinguish a person's qualities from the person's innermost self? Can't we only know what we see?"

The Earl raised his eyebrows and hesitated. He was by no means accustomed to philosophical discussion over his glass of *fino,* or at any other time, come to that. But he was saved having to answer by Anstruther who announced, "Dinner is served, my lord," and they all went into the dining room.

But Marianne, determined to show her uncle that she was not as empty-headed as he seemed to think, did not let the matter drop. Once the first course dishes had been served, she came back to it. "Anyway, what do you think, Uncle Giles? Do you think we can know a person other than by his or her qualities?"

His lordship, who had, in fact, been considering the matter, intrigued by the idea of these two women spending their afternoon sewing and discussing philosophy, replied, "I think we are always influenced by the visible qualities of a person, but our opinion must in the end be formed by their actions. Nanny used to say *handsome is as handsome does*. I suppose someone may look beautiful and have good intentions, which would be fine qualities, but for some reason or another perform foolish or even wicked actions. I think we would be likely to judge by that, not by their beauty or their intentions."

"But what if they were really sorry about it afterwards? That would be a fine quality. The vicar at home always taught us we should forgive others."

"We might forgive, but if the action had consequences that were very uncomfortable for others, especially for ourselves, I imagine we would nonetheless find it difficult to consider the person who caused them fine and good. But what do *you* think, Miss Drover? You are responsible, after all, for this discussion. I have no doubt you are possessed of very fine qualities, but by having Marianne translate and discuss Pascal, your actions have resulted in our dinner going cold while we talk. How are we to judge you?"

He said this with such humor in his eyes that Rosemary felt herself blushing.

"I hope, sir, that you would consider the unintended consequences of a cold dinner worth the fact that your ward spent her time this afternoon considering Pascal instead of the *Mysteries of Udolpho!*"

"Touché again, Miss Drover!" said his lordship with a smile. "You do seem to have the ability to put me in my place." So saying, he reflected that being put in his place by this transformed creature with her burnished hair, wide eyes (yes, they *were* blue) and white bosom was far different from a pert reply by an ugly woman in sackcloth. What would Pascal have to say about that, he wondered.

For her part, Rosemary did not know what to say. She was finding the Earl's smiling response harder to deal with than the ill humor she was accustomed to from him. Could a pretty dress and a new coiffure make so much difference? If that were so, his lordship must be very shallow indeed.

But Marianne was well satisfied with herself. "He didn't exactly laugh, but he *did* smile," she crowed as they went up to bed that night. "Do you know, I think he quite likes having us here. *Dear* Uncle Giles!" and she laughed merrily.

The next week followed the same pattern. The ladies breakfasted in their rooms, took a walk in the morning, and in the afternoon, Rosemary concentrated on unpicking and preparing of the materials for cutting out, Marianne, to her disgust, was forced to continue her studies. In the High House library they found a copy of Georg Forster's *A Voyage Around the World*, an account of a voyage with Captain Cook published in 1777. Rosemary directed her charge to identify on the globe (also located in the library) the Pacific Island he visited and to read out loud to her passages she found interesting, either from the accounts of life in the islands or the life on board the sloop *Resolution*. Marianne protested it would take *years* to read the many-volumed work, but since it was her governess's intention to keep her occupied for several days while, with the help of the visiting seamstress, she made her dresses, the protests fell on deaf ears.

"I shall turn into a positive antidote," moaned Marianne. "A bluestocking – like you! No one will want to marry me!"

"Nonsense!" replied Rosemary sternly. "No man who objects to his wife having a little learning is worth marrying!"

His lordship, who happened to enter the library just at that moment, said, "Quite right! You have no idea how irritating it is to have to listen to a constant babble of nothing when the initial attraction ... wears off."

He noticed Rosemary frowning at him and stopped abruptly, conscious once again of having said more than he should.

"But how can you know? You're not married, Uncle Giles!" protested Marianne, innocently.

"...Er, just so," said her uncle, in some confusion, "But," collecting himself. "That's why I'm not married. I've never found anyone ... learned enough."

Rosemary smiled down at her hands. She was quite sure that intellectual development was not his lordship's primary concern when choosing his female companions.

"You'd better marry Rosie, then," retorted Marianne. "She's learned enough for anyone. *And* she's pretty."

The Earl raised his eyebrows at this, and Miss Drover blushed in spite of herself. She had returned to what she now thought of as her sackcloth, having decided to wear her blue gown only at dinner until her other dresses were made, and she knew she looked decidedly unpretty.

Feeling a little foolish, she answered with more than a touch of asperity, "Don't be ridiculous, Marianne. And stop teasing his lordship. No one admires pertness in a girl."

His lordship said nothing.

Mrs. Croft, the seamstress, who arrived a couple of days after these activities had started, proved to be more than up to the challenge of helping to make gowns for one of the new young ladies at High House. Although she called herself Mrs., she had never been married. She was one of those unfortunate single women so often left to their own devices by the death of parents who had not been able to provide adequately for her future. Since she was handy with a needle, she had made a living travelling from one large estate to another doing the work that no one else had the time or the expertise to do.

She was a timid, self-effacing little woman and hers was not an easy lot. She was often poorly paid and ill-housed, and generally ignored as she quietly did her work. Much depended on the housekeeper, who was the one who hired her, for she was hardly ever seen above stairs. Like a governess, her place was neither downstairs nor upstairs. In many homes she worked and ate alone. She was always happy to come to High House, however, as Mrs. Brown treated her well, gave her a warm, well-lit place to work and invited her to sit with the staff at table. She enjoyed her meals in a company, which, under the stern eye of Mr. Anstruther, was not exactly joyous, but certainly more congenial than solitude. Thus, she was only too pleased to stay an extra few days, only requesting that a note be sent to her next destination to delay her arrival there.

She entered with enthusiasm into the plan for remaking her late ladyship's gowns, and exclaimed over the fineness of the fabrics. Accustomed as she was to dealing with cottons, coarse or fine, depending on their use, making up simple dresses for the maids and sometimes repairing the linens or upholstery, this represented a delightful change. Rosemary had already cut out the gowns she wanted and proposed that Mrs. Croft sit with her and Marianne to sew and listen to the geography lessons. That lady could hardly believe her good fortune and afterwards always regarded those few days spent with Miss Marianne and Miss Drover as some of the happiest in her life. She became so enthralled listening to the account of Forster's voyage that she sometimes forgot what she was doing and sat, mouth open in wonder.

"Just fancy!" she said, "Those natives greeting the sailors on the beach naked as the day they were born, and then poking under their clothes to see if they were men the same as them! And the behavior of the men and women together! It makes one blush to think about it!"

For, of course, Marianne had chosen the most salacious parts of the account to read aloud, and when Rosemary frowned dreadfully, exclaimed, "But you told me to pick out the passages that interested me the most! And I did read about the fish that shone in the moonlight. That was entirely unexceptionable!"

Soon enough, the three new gowns for Rosemary were ready, together with one for Marianne, made of a length of pale green silk found rolled up in one of the trunks. Mrs. Croft proved a genius at finding trim and lace that could be removed and repurposed, with the result that Marianne's dress had a pretty band of lace around the neck and puff sleeves, and Rosemary's dark blue velvet had black trim under the bosom and around the bottom of the skirt, about eight inches from the hem.

During the mornings while the ladies walked, Mrs. Croft made them petticoats from the white cotton kept for the maids' aprons, and refurbished the lining of the cloak with black silk generally used for the housekeeper's gowns. When she surveyed it all, Rosemary could hardly believe it. She had never had such a wardrobe in her life. However, other than the shapeless felt affair she had worn when she first came to take up her position in Fairfield Court, she still lacked a bonnet. But a further search of the trunks discovered a straw hat with a wide though somewhat worn and uneven brim, whose ribbons were sadly faded and frayed. But when these were removed and a wide strip of the blue velvet was fixed over the crown and tied under the ear, pulling down the side brims, it almost resembled a poke bonnet and Miss Drover declared herself well pleased.

Rosemary had written to Mrs. Hardcastle inviting her to tea the following Tuesday. The day dawned bright and clear, with no hint of the morning mists of the previous weeks, a sure sign that spring was fully upon them. The drawing room windows, with the curtains drawn back, gave a fine view of the sloping lawn, bordered at the top by flower beds, where daffodils now danced and the pursed lips of the tulips would open in a smile as the sun warmed them. She wore her amber silk for the first time, the color enhancing the chestnut of her hair and bringing out the grey-blue of her eyes. Marianne wore a pretty sprigged muslin printed with forget-me-nots, and a blue band in her fair hair. They were both in the best of looks and even Rosemary, who thought she should know better at her age, was excited to be receiving guests.

Their neighbor proved to be a stout matron, carefully corseted into an old-fashioned gown with wide skirts. Her daughter Mariah was just six months younger than Marianne, a slim, timid girl with a sandy complexion, dressed in a salmon pink that did not really become her. Her son Jasper, two years older, was home from Eton, and on his way to Oxford for the Michaelmas term. He was a youth of just over medium height, sandy like his sister, but with rather more worldly bronze from having been away at school. He was dressed in what was clearly the London style, with slim buff pantaloons, shining boots, a striped waistcoat and a well-tailored coat of navy superfine. His neckcloth was tied carefully in a complicated design and his starched shirt collar was perhaps a trifle too high. He appeared to have come prepared to be bored by the company of women and was inclined to be rigid, but when Marianne greeted him with her best smile there was a distinct thaw in his standoffishness.

"There now," said his Mama. "Didn't I say as Miss Marianne was bound to be a pretty girl, her uncle being as good-looking as he is. To be sure, he has had more caps set at him than any man in these parts. And I doubt not that Miss Marianne will have her share of admirers, too. You will steal a march on them, Jasper, by knowing her first!"

"Why, Ma'am," said Marianne, her natural exuberance a sharp contrast to Mariah Hardcastle's quiet demeanor, "are there many other families in the neighborhood?"

"My dear! We are a tidy little circle here," cried Mrs. Hardcastle, who Rosemary soon recognized as the neighborhood gossip and town crier. "The Smythes are only three miles to the east. They have one boy up at Cambridge. I believe he is up in town this summer. Their younger boy is about eight. He will be away at school in the autumn. Then the Pendletons over the hill have a baby boy born a couple of months ago and twin daughters, identical and impossible to tell apart. Not yet fourteen and always ready for a romp! Poor Lucy Mannering down the road from us is a widow. Her husband was killed in the Peninsular war, you know, so sad. She has just the one boy, Christopher, home from Eton at the moment, same as Jasper. The two of them are thick as thieves, always out, up to no good, frightening the sheep and scrumping the apples."

"Mother! Please!" exclaimed Jasper, very conscious of his dignity. "We haven't done such a thing for years! Anyone would think we were still boys!"

"And so you are, my dear, and very naughty boys, too," she continued, sublimely unaware of the giggle from Marianne and the annoyed look on her son's face. "Then there's General and Mrs. Broadbent, too of course, but they are older. He is not in very prime twig, by all accounts. Had a bad time with his liver over the winter, I understand. Spent several years in India, so it's not surprising." She mused for a moment. "I know! I have the very thing! I shall arrange a dinner party for us all, so that you may meet the neighbors. I shan't invite the eight-year old, of course, and strictly speaking, neither Miss Marianne nor Mariah is out yet, and the Pendleton girls are full young, but we are all good friends. No one will stand on ceremony. It will be good for them to have to put on company manners."

"Oh, dear Madam, what a wonderful idea!" cried Marianne. "We should enjoy it above all things, shouldn't we, Rosie?"

"It does sound very appealing, if you are sure, Mrs. Hardcastle, that we are not imposing upon you?"

"Imposing? Nonsense! Nothing I like more than guests around my table. Now tell me, Miss Drover, how are you finding our Kentish Weald?"

The maids circulated with plates of dainty sandwiches and tartlets and Rosemary poured the tea, which Jasper carried to Marianne and his sister, receiving a smile from the one and whispered thanks from the other. While Rosemary and the matron chatted politely, if somewhat uninterestingly, Jasper wasted no time in talking to Marianne. She, for her part, remembering Rosemary's strict instructions to make sure no one sat silent and apart, did her best to engage Mariah, so that the three of them were soon sitting companionably engaged in a discourse that clearly amused them all to judge from the occasional bursts of laughter.

The small party was just breaking up when the Earl came in. He had clearly forgotten that they were to receive visitors that day, though Rosemary had sought his permission and informed him of the details. He managed to cover his surprise at finding his drawing room full of chattering people and bowed politely to Mrs. Hardcastle.

Marianne leaped up when she saw him and ran over saying, "Uncle Giles! We have been talking about the neighbors and Mrs. Hardcastle is inviting us to a dinner party to meet them all! Isn't that kind?"

His lordship's eyebrows rose. "It certainly is." And turning to that lady, said, "Please do not feel obliged to do so. I should have thought of it myself, but I'm afraid I have little experience of such things."

"Indeed, and why should you, a single man, used to living his own life and suddenly having two young ladies to entertain? To be sure, no one would expect it."

"And," Marianne was clearly determined to press the advantage of an audience. "I've been telling Jasper and Mariah (Miss Drover noticed that the move to Christian names had already been effected), that Rosie is writing a play for us to perform in the ruined chapel. They are just dying to take part, so please say we may do it, dear Uncle Giles!"

Dear Uncle Giles looked taken aback at this full-frontal attack. He rose to it valiantly, nonetheless. "It is for Mrs. Hardcastle to give her permission, if …er Miss and Mr. Hardcastle (he had obviously not bothered to remember their names) are to perform, but," he hesitated, "otherwise I have no objection."

Deliberately ignoring the frown Rosemary had given her when she launched her sally at the Earl, Marianne clapped her hands delightedly. "Oh, Mrs. Hardcastle I'm sure has no objection," she cried. "I feel I know her already for a good sport!"

Mrs. Hardcastle laughed, quite flattered at being considered a good sport by so lively a young lady. "If Miss Drover is to be the author and oversee the whole, there can be no objection," she agreed.

And so it was decided. The Earl felt himself run over by superior forces and reflected, as he bowed his way out of the drawing room, that he had underestimated the effect of having his ward and her companion in his home. He was already aware of a different atmosphere in High House. The laughter and animated discussions of his ward and her companion could often be heard where before there had been silence. Mealtimes were far from the formal events he had been accustomed to, and the piano music Rosemary often afforded them in the evenings rang throughout the house, to the obvious pleasure of everyone, even those in the kitchens.

Marianne had a youthful vitality that had yet to be subdued by the decorum required of a London Season. Miss Drover, while gently urging her to restrain her excesses and requiring her to spend at least part of the day in some sort of study, did not try to completely dampen the enthusiasm that in many ways was the basis of her charm. As a result, Miss Marianne was popular with everyone, from the cook who was delighted to receive her warm, not to say exaggerated, compliments, to Anstruther, the butler, whose arm she took confidentially to whisper that it was *such* a relief to see his calm face whenever she came home. It was the first time his lordship had observed at close hand the education of a young gentlewoman, and while he thought Marianne still had much to learn about decorum, he recognized that Miss Drover demonstrated just the right combination of governess and friend. He had to admit that he was impressed by her.

Chapter Eight

The day of Mrs. Hardcastle's dinner party arrived and there was as much frenzy at High House as was possible for a well-run household led by a man who liked a quiet, ordered life. The new pale green silk dress made for Marianne from the material found in the attic was found to be rather too long, as she had worn higher heels when trying it on. Rosemary effected last minute alterations. But that required careful pressing on a day when the irons had not been put in the fire and caused a flurry in the kitchens.

The color of the gown was perfect with Marianne's brown eyes and fair hair, which was drawn back from her pretty face and fell in ringlets from a rosette at the back of her head.

Rosemary's own beaded violet lustring, which she wore for the first time, fitted her slim shape to perfection but caused her some anxiety. Entirely by accident, it had been cut rather lower than the other gowns, and she was unused to seeing her white bosom so much displayed. She was inclined to change her gown, but Marianne persuaded her that the color became her so well, and made her eyes look so blue, that it would be a pity not to wear it. In the end, Mrs. Brown suggested using a strip of the leftover fabric, folded and pressed (since the irons were now hot) into tiny pleats and sewn around the neckline. This provided just another inch of coverage and satisfied Rosemary's modesty.

She brushed her hair up and fastened her curls on the top of her head. She did not possess any sort of headdress but had had the forethought to cover with a scrap of white lace a narrow, curved whalebone taken from the waist of one of the cannibalized dresses. She was able to use this as a hairband with her curls looped in and out. The effect was very pretty. With her pearls and a pair of lace gloves discovered in the attic trunk, yellow with age but bleached white, she was ready.

They came downstairs to find his lordship waiting. He was dressed plainly in slim trousers, a long waisted jacket cut away over a sober fitted waistcoat and a neckcloth in unostentatious folds fastened with a diamond pin. While nothing about him stood out in the least degree, he looked uncommonly fine. His jacket, while not molded to his broad shoulders in a way that would have required the help of two men to get him into it, fit him to perfection. His shirt collars were starched to precisely the right degree and his neckcloth was folded with elegance if not with complexity. Rosemary surprised herself by a feeling of pride as he handed her into the carriage and rode with them to the party. She and Marianne would certainly be arriving with the best-looking man in the area.

For his part, the Earl was as gratified as he could be, accompanying two very pretty ladies to what promised to be an insipid affair. He had maintained a polite but distant relationship with his neighbors and usually contrived to be in London when social events were arranged. He discovered now that his instinct had been right to do so. The gentlemen seemed to hold him somewhat in awe, but their wives lost no time in renewing their acquaintance with him. He listened to Mrs. Smythe describe the academic achievement at Cambridge of her older boy, who appeared to be a scholar of enormous promise, and heard from Mrs. Pendleton the wildly funny things the twins had recently uttered, together with the assertion that her infant son was the most intelligent child nanny had ever seen. Her husband said nothing, but stood ogling Miss Drover. Mrs. Mannering, the widow of the Peninsular war, was quick to work her way to his side as soon as he was alone. She was a curvaceous brunette with dimples, accustomed to hear herself described as a handsome woman. She swept him a curtsey low enough for him to be able to look down the front of her dress. Unlike Rosemary, she had no problem displaying her charms.

"My lord," she said, as she rose, looking up at him between her lashes. "It's been an age since we saw you at one of our gatherings. One would almost think you deliberately avoided us!"

"Not at all, Mrs. …er, Mannering. I'm afraid business in town often forces me to absent myself."

"Well, we must make the most of you now that you're here, mustn't we?" She smiled engagingly. "I daresay you do not recognize my boy Christopher. He is so much grown these last months."

She waved her fan towards a youth who had wasted no time in joining his friend Jasper talking animatedly to Marianne. He was a stocky youth, dark like his mother, with a good deal of self-assurance. Mariah, who stood off to one side, was stealing admiring glances at him, when she was not looking down at her gloves.

"He seems to have already made a conquest," remarked his lordship.

"Oh, he is as yet just a boy, though I must say, he has a great deal of address. He's due to go up to Oxford with Jasper, of course. I don't know how I shall go on without him! It is a lonely life for a widow, you know." She looked at him sorrowfully.

He forbore to answer that since her son had been several years at Eton, she must be well able to go on without him. Recognizing this as a ploy for him to offer her relief from her loneliness, his lordship offered no reply other than, "I'm sure, Madam." After a moment, he bowed and moved off, saying that he should greet their hostess.

It was, frankly, an unconventional gathering. None of the young ladies was yet out. The not quite fourteen-year-old girl twins were only just out of childhood and Mariah and Marianne were only a year older. It was for all of them their first sortie into an adult party and they were conscious of it. The two young men, having finished at Eton, were inclined to think themselves adult, but they naturally preferred to socialize with the young ladies rather than with their mothers and their cronies. The gentlemen were too old like the General, too much family men like Mr. Smythe and Mr. Pendleton, or, like the Earl, too frighteningly superior. It had not been an easy table to arrange, and in the end, Mrs. Hardcastle had placed all the young people at one end and the adults at the other. It was testimony to her kindness as a hostess that she sat herself at the young peoples' end, thus condemning herself to being surrounded by a good deal of chatter uninteresting to anyone over the age of seventeen.

However, Marianne, remembering Rosemary's strict instructions to make sure no one in her orbit was left out, soon engaged her hostess in a variety of topics, from what fashion trends would likely endure, to whether she preferred the ballet to the opera, not forgetting the weather (what climactic conditions she might expect to find in that part of Kent). Consequently, their hostess was left with a very favorable impression of that young lady's mind and manners. She later complimented her guardian, who, to do him justice, gave all the credit to Miss Drover.

The Earl had other reasons to give the governess credit. She had been seated opposite him and he had watched her carry on a deft conversation on her right with the General, who, combining indifferent health with a degree of deafness and a pompous certainty that he was the most consequential person in the room, was never easy to talk to. On her left was Mr. Pendleton, father of the girl twins. He appeared to think this gave him the right to adopt an attitude towards her that was half way between avuncular and suggestive. He asked her about her beaux and when she blushingly protested, raised an eyebrow, saying he would show her around town when she was next in London. She thanked him with a smile but said firmly that she did not expect to be in London any time soon.

Both men also complimented the Earl on his choice of governess-companion.

"Pretty gel," said the General later, over the port. "Well informed and not too pleased with herself to talk to an old man."

"Where did you find *her*, you lucky dog," was Mr. Pendleton's comment. "I'd like a governess like that for my two. Couldn't let me have her, could you? Your ward's no longer needing a governess, surely."

"Perhaps not," replied his lordship, "but she is now acting as chaperone and companion. Besides, the two are sincerely attached since the death of both Marianne's mother and father. I could not think of separating them."

"Nice excuse to keep her around, I must say," came the response. "But, as I say, if things change, let me know."

To this, the Earl vouchsafed no answer, but merely inclined his head. He himself had been obliged to talk to the General's wife on his right and Mrs. Mannering on his left. It had not been undiluted delight. The General's wife concentrated on her husband's glorious career in India, and interlarded her comments with references to Government House and the Club, which seemed to have occupied all her time. Mrs. Mannering, pressing her arm against his, continued to speak in a confiding tone about her sad situation and how empty her life would be without Her Boy, all the while dimpling up at him and presenting her buxom charms for his inspection. When he asked whether she had no acquaintance in London or even Bath with whom she might spend a few days when Her Boy was away, she raised large brown eyes to his face and said, "A widow alone is poor company and one does so miss the company of a man when one travels. A real man, that is, on whom one can depend. Besides, I could not bear to leave the memories of my dear husband that surround me here."

The Earl privately thought that if any sort of man with a reasonable fortune made her the offer of any sort of company, she would leave her memories and Her Boy without a backward glance, but, of course, he did not say so.

When the men, including Jasper and Christopher who, to their delight, were considered men enough to stay with the port, joined the ladies in the drawing room, the young ladies were already at one end of the room setting up a game of spillikins. Very much on their dignity, the two young men joined them, standing off to the side at first. But after a while, they could not resist joining in, so that the game, which occasioned short periods of extreme quiet while the spills were extracted, was soon loud with shouts and crowing when they fell. There was desultory conversation amongst the adults and his lordship was thinking about how soon his party could beat a polite retreat, when Marianne, who had been knocked out of the game, approached their hostess with the suggestion that they ask Rosemary to play.

"She often plays for us at High House in the evenings. She's really very good!"

Miss Drover was at once begged to entertain them and, after it became clear that none of the other ladies or girls had any desire to exhibit, she sat, a little reluctantly, at the piano.

"I see there is quite a collection of country airs and songs here," she said, thumbing through the music, "so that is what I shall play."

"But you don't need the music!" protested Marianne. "You know lots of things by heart. You know you do!"

Conscious from the slight frown she gave Marianne that her governess had no desire to show herself as any sort of virtuoso, his lordship surprised them both by speaking up.

"Let Miss Drover play what she wishes, Marianne. Unless you wish to entertain us yourself?"

This effectively silenced his ward's protests, and Rosemary began to play, softly at first, so that conversation and the spillikins game could continue. After a few pieces, she began to sing. Her voice was sweet and tuneful, and it was not long before the room fell silent listening to her. His lordship found he could not take his eyes off her. The branched chandelier on the piano set flame in her hair, the beads in her violet gown winked in the candlelight, her eyes were darkest blue as she looked down under her lashes, and her white throat, with the delicate row of pearls, rose and fell with her voice.

"By God," he heard Pendleton mutter, "she's a beauty!" For once, the Earl found himself in total agreement with his neighbor.

Rosemary played and sang for over an hour, during the last part of which, the young people and some of the adults joined in.

Rosemary played rounds, which at first caused hilarious protests when the young men persisted in coming in at the wrong moment. But when all the parts were properly managed, the assembled company performed very creditably. Even the General, once he understood what was going on, participated in a rather tuneless bellow, and the Earl surprised everyone, including himself, with his pleasant baritone.

It was almost midnight when the party broke up, Mr. Pendleton declaring that the night was young, his wife protesting that the girls should be in bed and the young men making last minute arrangements to call for Marianne the following afternoon to take her and Mariah for a drive. Mrs. Hardcastle declared that the evening had been the most pleasant anyone could remember.

"*Dear* Uncle Giles!" cried Marianne, once they were in the carriage. "Thank you, thank you a million times. I have never had so much fun in my life!" She yawned luxuriously.

"It's Miss Drover you should thank," replied her uncle. "It was she who saved the evening from being a dead bore. Before she started to play, I was wondering how soon we could leave."

"In truth, it's Mrs. Hardcastle who deserves our gratitude," said Rosemary. "She is the sort of hostess who appears to do nothing, but quietly makes sure everyone is happy. You would do well to observe her, Marianne. It is a trick every woman who is likely to be in the role of hostess should learn."

"Oh, dear Rosie, trust you to make a lesson out of it!" said Marianne. "When I'm a hostess I shall make sure everyone has lots of lovely food and champagne and that will make them happy!"

"Throw in a few people worth talking to," replied his lordship, "and you may have found the perfect formula. Which reminds me, you have both received compliments this evening: Mrs. Hardcastle finds you, Marianne, to be possessed of both a good mind and good manners, and the General finds you well informed, Miss Drover. I was congratulated on my excellent choice of a governess for my ward, congratulations I graciously accepted but did not merit in the least, as I had nothing to do with it." He did not mention Pendleton's comments.

"But you did have the sense, dear Uncle Giles," said Marianne, "to let Rosie come with me to High House."

"I wasn't aware I had a choice," was the dampening reply. "And please stop calling me *dear Uncle Giles*. Just *Giles* will do."

"It most certainly will not!" said Rosemary at once. "I insist that Marianne show proper respect to her elders. *Uncle Giles* or *my lord* is proper. She should by all means drop the *dear*."

"Are you sure then, Miss Drover," murmured the Earl, and there was a distinct smile in his voice, though it was too dark to see his face, "that she should be calling you *dear Rosie*? Does that meet your exacting standards?"

"But she *is* my dear Rosie," came Marianne's by now sleepy voice, "and no one else's."

Miss Drover reached over and squeezed her hand, and his lordship reflected to himself that unfortunately, that was true.

Chapter Nine

The performance of a play in the ruined chapel now seemed to be an accepted thing and Marianne implored Rosemary to write one as quickly as could be. Had Rosemary not prevented it, her charge would have been taken up every afternoon, and morning too, by visits, drives and walks with Mariah, with whom Marianne soon became bosom-bows, and, more often than not, with Jasper and Christopher. Mrs. Hardcastle was, fortunately, insistent on the proprieties and would not let Mariah out without a chaperone, even when her brother was with her.

"For," as she said, "he is, after all, nothing but a silly boy and if some opportunity for sport comes his way, is likely to forget to look after her as he should."

The chaperone was the nanny's assistant, a sort of children's maid, who had helped look after them when they, and she, were very young. She had not been more than fourteen when she had been engaged, and was now a little over thirty years old, a cheerful, unflappable woman of only moderate understanding, but who was like a mother-hen as far as Mariah, her darling, was concerned. Her status in the house was unclear, except that she knew where everything was, was happy to undertake any task and run any errand. She would sit behind the girls in the carriage, get down to open and close every gate, walk behind them when they strolled along the lanes, and remonstrate good humoredly with the young men. They often proved Mrs. Hardcastle's assessment of them correct, choosing to swing from low hanging branches as the carriage drove underneath or run along the top of the walls as the girls walked by. The advantage of this arrangement was that Rosemary could safely leave Marianne in her care and spend an afternoon alone now and then, quietly reading, practicing the piano or thinking about the dratted play in the ruins.

She was determined, however, that no play would be produced unless it could be an opportunity for Marianne to learn something. They read Sophocles' *Oedipus Rex* and talked about the structure of drama, with its exposition, complication and resolution. Then Rosemary sent her off to decide on a topic and to present ideas on how it could be done. Marianne pouted for two days, and then realized that at this rate, nothing would be achieved, so bent her mind to the task. Her first suggestions were, naturally, of a chilling gothic nature, concerning unhappy orphaned young women carried off by a wicked uncle and rescued from a locked tower by a handsome hero on a snow-white charger. *The Mysteries of Udolpho* all over again. But Rosemary pointed out that, apart from being insulting to her uncle, who, far from locking her in a tower, allowed her to do pretty much as she pleased, it was beyond their capacities to stage a play as proposed by Marianne.

"Think of the Greeks and *Oedipus,*" she said. "No towers, no horses, no scenery. That's what we need. The ruins themselves should be all the background we need. How about something from history? Is there a person who interests you?"

Marianne finally came running in one day crying "Mary Queen of Scots! She's perfect. She spent most of her life locked up in one place or another and then she had her head chopped off. She can be thinking about her life and various people can appear. We can make a gory head out of a cabbage, or something! It will be horrible and wonderful!"

So that was it. Rosemary found the suggestion altogether suitable and sat down at once to write the play. Once it was completed, she decided she should obtain the approval of the Earl before they went any further and accordingly sought him out in his study a few days later.

"I'm afraid, my lord," she said, "Marianne is very taken with the idea of a play in the ruins. And you did, perhaps in a moment of weakness, agree that it could be done. She has actually worked hard to come up with a suitable topic, and I have written it. Here it is for your approval. I hope you will find it appropriate. It has a reasonable amount of gore, to keep the interest of the public!"

"Good God! And who are the public? Are we to sell tickets?"

Rosemary laughed. "No, of course not, but Marianne and her friends have been talking about it for weeks now and everyone knows about it. I thought we could invite all the neighbors one afternoon and then have tea. I imagine the mothers will all come, and perhaps the fathers. The servants may be given leave to watch it. It's quite short. We need not trouble you at all, indeed, you don't even have to come!"

"My reputation for being a surly and unwelcoming neighbor is bad enough already. If I don't come to a play in my own grounds it will be sunk beyond repair! Leave it with me and I'll read it before dinner. By the way, Miss Drover, I have enjoyed hearing you practicing that very pretty piece on the piano. What is it?"

"It's by an Italian composer called Vivaldi, from his composition called *The Four Seasons,* the part describing Spring. He didn't write it for the piano at all. He was a violinist. I didn't know of it, but there was an article about it in *The Times*. Someone played a piece arranged for piano at a concert, and the article said it was very lovely, so I sent for a copy of the music. I look at the newspaper most days. I've asked Anstruther to put the newspaper aside for me, when you're finished with it. I hope you don't mind? It's such a treat. We hardly ever had newspapers at Fairchild Court and here you have them every day."

"Why should I mind? I'm delighted you enjoy reading it. I'm amazed you've had time to write a play on top of everything else."

"Oh, the play is a silly nothing. It only took a couple of hours. The best part, really, is that Marianne did a good deal of work on the topic. Now that she has friends in the neighborhood, she hardly has time for anything else. I'm afraid my influence over her is coming to an end. I only hope I have given her what she needs, in terms of not only an education, but also how to go on in the world, because my days as a governess are all but over. Now if I can just see her married to a man who will love and look after her, I shall be happy."

"And have you no such ambition for yourself, Miss Drover?" asked his lordship, surprised and not a little touched that so personable a young woman should think only of the girl in her charge.

Rosemary laughed. "Oh no! Who would want to marry a penniless governess? Or, perhaps I should say, who would want to marry me that I should care to accept? I have no intention of becoming nurse to a demanding older gentleman, or unpaid housekeeper to a younger one. My hope is that Marianne will keep me with her, and that at length I shall become governess to her children. That is the best outcome for me. And I have my books and my music, after all."

"She will be fortunate indeed if that comes to pass," commented his lordship. "I have rarely met a woman with a mind as well developed as yours. You will be wasted on a parcel of brats!"

"I don't see it in that light. You will remember our disagreement on the value of education for women. I still maintain that an educated mother, or, in our case, both mother and governess, make for an educated man. If the children should happen to include a future government minister or leader of some sort, or even if he is just a fair-minded head of his own family, I shall consider it a worthy way to have spent my life."

So saying, Rosemary honored the Earl with a brief curtsey and left him. He sat at his desk for some time thinking over what she had said, and at last turned to the paper in his hand.

The Last Days of Mary, Queen of Scots

Dramatis personae
Mary: Marianne
Darnley: Jasper
James: the Smythe's young son (*I hope*)
Bothwell: Christopher
Elizabeth: one of the twins
Executioner: Jasper (he will have time to change)
Silent Chorus (*Scene Notice Carrier*): Mariah (*she is too shy to have a speaking part*)

Act The First

Silent Chorus crosses the stage bearing a notice:
Chartley Manor 1585

Mary is asleep in her bedchamber. She dreams.
Enter Darnley, pale and wearing a shroud.
Mary *as if in a dream*: Darnley! My love! Whence comes this lifeless pallor?
Darnley: If any soul knowest how I died, 'tis thee, most treacherous wife! I lay upon my sickbed while thou didst disport thyself in dance and feasting. There came one who did place a pillow on my face and I, too weak to move, did lose my breath, and life.
Mary: No, my love, not I! Upon my own life I declare I did not seek thy death!
Darnley leaves. Enter a child, wearing a crown and a royal cloak, too big and long for him.
Mary: James! My babe, my own!
James: Must I be king, mother? I am too small to bear this crown.
Mary: Aye, until I return to Scotland with the crown of England on mine head, our two kingdoms thus to join.
The child leaves. Enter Bothwell, dressed as a courtier, with a glass of wine in his hand.
Mary: Bothwell! Thou traitor! Upon the field of battle thou didst my side betray. When I was taken, where wert thou? And what knowest thou of Darnley's death? I fear he too by you was treason'd.
Bothwell: Unhappy woman! Bethink thyself! It is not thyself a man would seek, but the glory of thy crown! If Darnley died it was for cause. He was too weak and not a man. I did thy side uphold until thou wast taken by thy foes. I cared not to follow thee into imprisonment.
Bothwell leaves.

Act The Second

Mary wakes up, arises from her bed and using a walking stick, goes to a chair and takes up her embroidery. Enter Queen Elizabeth.

Mary: (*rising and using her walking stick to assist her making a curtsey*) My Cousin and my Queen!
Eliz.: Mary! How canst thou work thy needle in this gloom?
Mary: I need no light. My fingers do the work themselves. My mind forsooth is elsewhere.
Eliz.: Upon what dost thou ponder?
Mary: Upon my beloved Darnley, traitorously slain. And Bothwell, who upon the field of battle did most cowardly flee. And upon James, my son, too young to bear the crown his head did hold when he was but a babe, and, as I believe, his allegiance to his mother now forsworn.
Eliz.: I sorrow that thy memories be not softer, for I fear thy future life be harder still.
Mary: Why speakest thou so? Save thy love, little enough of joy surrounds me here. I am imprisoned in this house, while my failing body holds me to this chamber.
Eliz.: False cousin! I know thou workest stratagems against me. My Lord Walsingham hath shown me letters thou hast writ wherein you seek my throne, my head withal.
Mary: (*Rising to her feet painfully with her cane*) My Queen! I am most villainously betrayed. How canst thou think that I, crippled as I am, can seek thy crown?
Eliz: My counselors do not lie. Philip of Spain stands ready to support thee with his troops, and the Pope himself doth propose for you a marriage to this Spaniard's

brother. Thou art accused of treason. See if at trial thou canst thyself excuse!
Exit Queen Elizabeth.

Act The Third

Silent Chorus passes across the stage bearing a notice:
The Trial of Mary, Fotheringay Castle, 1586

Mary stands and faces the audience.

Mary: My Lords, I stand before ye, a woman accused but alone. I have no lawyer, nor yet am I allowed my books and papers. Ye accuse me of treason, but how can this be? I am no English subject, but anointed Queen of Scotland and, until the death of my beloved husband Francis, Queen of France. Look to your conscience and remember that the world is wider than this kingdom.
Voices offstage: Guilty! She is guilty of treason to the crown!
Mary is led to the execution block. Her cloak is removed, and she is shown in a white gown. The executioner kneels for her forgiveness.
Mary: I forgive thee with all my heart, for now, I hope, thou wilt make an end to all my troubles.
She kneels down, her back towards the audience and places her head over the block, so that it is invisible to the audience. The executioner raises his axe and strikes once, twice, three times. He finally lifts up her bloody head and shows the audience.
Executioner: God Save The Queen!

FINIS

The Earl's eyebrows rose and he chuckled as he imagined the reaction of the audience to the grisly "head". He promised himself to be there for the performance, even if it meant taking tea with his neighbors. That evening at dinner, therefore, he gave his ward permission to perform in the ruined chapel with her friends and said he was looking forward to it. Afterwards, Rosemary played the Vivaldi to enthusiastic acclaim from both her listeners and they all went to bed in the greatest charity with each other.

During the following weeks, Rosemary and Marianne worked on the play. It was first necessary to persuade the participants to take the parts they had been allocated. The Smythe youngster was all for it. He saw it as an opportunity to be in the company of Jasper and Christopher, who were his heroes. The twins wanted very much to appear but argued incessantly as to which one should take the part. Since they were as alike as two peas, it made no difference to anyone but themselves. The problem was only resolved when Rosemary made them draw lots and promised the loser that she could still be on stage as Elizabeth's lady in waiting, carrying her train. This was at first met with scorn.

"What? I carry her train? I should think not, indeed!" cried the loser, who however, was finally persuaded that it was that or nothing.

She then spent the rehearsals attempting different ways to upstage Elizabeth, until Rosemary sternly told her that a lady in waiting did not walk in front of the queen, nor execute a series of pirouettes and grimaces that made her look like a performing monkey.

The two young men threw themselves into their roles with more enthusiasm than artistry and seemed to think their parts an opportunity for comedy. They certainly made each other laugh. Rosemary could only hope that stage fright would calm them down on the day. Marianne was the only performer who took her part seriously, learned her lines before anyone else and generally acted in such a responsible fashion that her governess found herself dependent on her to control the others.

The attics were raided for costumes, and Rosemary and Mrs. Croft, who had returned to High House at a most opportune moment, were able to make very creditable gowns for Mary and Elizabeth. Darnley would wear a white shroud fashioned out of a sheet found in the attics, where it had been stored because it had worn too thin to be of practical use. He had to be persuaded not to put it over his head and wail like a ghost. Instead, his hair and face would be powdered with a box of Sweet Cyprus Hair Powder, a product from fifty years before, found almost intact in the attic trunks. Then, as the executioner, he would simply pull over his head a black stocking with eyes cut out and don a grimy apron borrowed from the estate workshops. Bothwell would wear his own breeches, shirt and top boots, with the addition of a stiff embroidered bodice from one of the old dresses fashioned into a doublet. He was at first extremely loathe to wear what had been an item of women's clothing, and his friend chaffed him unmercifully. But when he saw how well it looked, he was persuaded, especially when a soft felt hat with a long, curled feather, of which no one seemed to know the origins, was produced. Then he wore his costume willingly and with a decided air.

A week of cloudy skies and pouring rain followed by days of drizzle delayed the performance of this oeuvre, which, by the time the young people had spread the word far and near, looked as if it would be attended by everyone anyone knew in the neighborhood and beyond. The cook and her assistants were much put out, never knowing from one day to the next if they should begin the baking for the tea. Finally, however, a period of settled skies presented itself. Rosemary declared the performance would be the day after next and sent notes to all the households in the area. She was heartily sick of it by this time, between Marianne running to the window asking did she not see the blue sky just over there, and surely it meant the rain was clearing, and the cook wringing her hands, saying that if she had to take out her baking trays and put them away one more time, she would have a Fatal Spasm.

On the day of the performance, the footmen had carried all the chairs from the ballroom downhill to the ruins, the maids had swept the chancel of bird droppings and leaves and the cook had finally filled her baking pans when, about midday, they received the devastating news that the two young men would be unable to perform. They had that morning been indulging in their favorite pastime of running along the top of the walls that flanked the Hardcastle estate, when they had been surprised by a pheasant shooting from its covert and had fallen headlong into a large bed of tall stinging nettles. Their hands and faces, and more particularly their eyelids, had been quite viciously stung, and all the application of mashed dock leaves in the world had not reduced the swelling. The doctor had been called and had advised their remaining quietly in their beds with the blinds down and cold compresses on their eyes. He had given them a small dose of laudanum and they were presently sleeping. There was no possibility of their performing that day.

It was impossible to change the arrangements. People would be arriving in under three hours. With Marianne wailing and her head in a spin, Rosemary made a rapid decision. Luckily, she had kept both young men's costumes at High House, not trusting them to remember them. She sent a note to Mrs. Hardcastle, asking her to send over a shirt and breeches, possibly something Jasper had grown out of. She would play the parts herself. When she told Marianne what she had decided, that young lady was torn between gratitude and being scandalized.

"You're going to appear in public in *breeches*?" she gasped. "But, but ... how will you *change*?" She looked horrified.

"Don't refine upon it dear," replied Rosemary with more calm than she felt. "It will just be for a moment. I just have to wear the breeches for Bothwell. He's the only one seen in normal men's clothing. And as for changing, I won't have to, really. I shall go down to the ruins in the breeches under my Darnley shroud, with my cloak over all. I shall go behind one of the pillars and take off my cloak. I can play Darnley, then I have only to remove the shroud to play Bothwell. That's the only time I'll be seen in breeches. Afterwards I'll don the apron for the Executioner. It will work, I assure you. The good news is that his lordship told me yesterday he will not be able to see the play, as he has urgent business with one of his tenants. Something to do with flooding after all this rain. I was a little disappointed, but now I'm delighted. Say nothing to him, for heaven's sake!"

Marianne was sufficiently reassured to be able to face his lordship later without a tremor, and when he offered his apologies for missing the performance, said with tolerable equanimity, "Oh, it's only a silly amusement for children, after all! You may be happy to be missing it."

The time for the performance arrived. The performers hid behind the chapel pillars and the audience took their seats. The servants from High House stood behind the chairs. They had been agog at all the preparations and what they had seen of the rehearsals. They had obtained the housekeeper's permission to leave their posts to watch the play, provided they hurried back to serve the guests at tea.

Rosemary rang a bell she had borrowed for the purpose. When the audience quieted, Marianne came forward and announced the title of the piece, then arranged herself on a low draped table serving as her bed. Her head up, as she had been instructed, Mariah walked across as the silent chorus with her notice, and they were off. Rosemary had powdered her hair and face. She dropped her cloak behind a pillar and stepped forward in her shroud. There was a little stir, as it became clear who was playing the part, but it soon quieted as she spoke out in a low, carrying voice. With a dignified gesture, she accused Mary of murdering her.

The Smythe boy came next and did well, hesitating a little at first, but then speaking out boldly and clearly. During that time, Rosemary quickly stripped off the sheet. As she bent to step out of it and to shake the powder from her hair, she was observed from behind by the Earl, who had completed his business more quickly than expected and had returned with more enthusiasm than he would have imagined to see the entertainment. He strode swiftly down the hill, quite by chance approaching at an angle that allowed him to see behind the pillar where Rosemary was effecting her change. He did not at first realize what he was seeing, but then recognized her and stopped abruptly to admire her shapely derriere as she bent in the rather tight breeches, for Mrs. Hardcastle had sent over a pair that Jasper had long outgrown. Luckily, Rosemary did not see him, or she would have hesitated before slipping into the embroidered doublet and jamming the feathered hat upon her head. As it was, she came onto the stage and carried off the part of Bothwell with enormous verve, her tone insinuating and insulting, a complete contrast to Darnley. The audience, by now into the story, certainly recognized her, but they were too entranced by the performance to wonder at it.

It was only as she was leaving the stage that her eye fell upon the Earl and her heart gave a leap. Whether she was glad to see him, or embarrassed that he saw her, she could not afterwards tell, and anyway, she was too busy changing herself into the Executioner to think about it. Queen Elizabeth and her lady made their entrance. After all their histrionics during rehearsals, the twins were inclined to look down and fail to project, until Rosemary hissed at them to look at the audience and for the queen to speak up. Mariah crossed the scene for the third Act, and the trial and execution scenes began.

Without telling the other performers, Rosemary had arranged that there would be a pan of red paint behind the black draped stool that served as the execution block. When the axe, a realistic looking instrument with a blade made of heavy card fitted onto a broomstick, came down to cut the head three times, this, by historical account, being the number of strokes required to sever Mary's head, it came up with red along its blade. There was a collective gasp, both from the audience and the other actors. Then, before raising the severed head, a gory affair made of papier mâché, she dipped it in the pan too, so that when she held it aloft, it dripped in a lifelike grisly fashion. One or two of the housemaids screamed and the audience murmured in delicious horror.

The performance was greeted with enormous acclaim. The Smythes were delighted with their lad's performance and, ignoring or forgetting the hours Rosemary had spent with him to get him to stand up straight and enunciate clearly, seemed to think it was all his own doing. Mrs. Pendleton was pleased with her daughters in spite of their lackluster performance, while Mr. Pendleton was pleased with the sight of Rosemary in breeches. Like the Earl, he had not failed to notice her bottom. He sought her out, but she, quickly donning her cloak and running up the hill, managed to avoid everyone. She went straight to her bedchamber, quickly brushed the rest of the powder out of her hair and changed into a gown. By the time she came down again, the guests had gathered in the drawing room and the tea was being brought in.

"Ah, Miss Drover," remarked the Earl, seeing her. "I hope you will act as hostess and pour the tea?" he made no mention of the breeches.

Rosemary was both astonished and flattered. She had planned to ask Mrs. Hardcastle to act as hostess. She knew that by asking her, his lordship had elevated her status in the household. She inclined her head and went immediately to the silver pots of tea and hot water. She was glad to do it, less for the distinction it gave her, than because it prevented her having to deal with all the questions and comments that her performance would inevitably bring. She had already noticed Mr. Pendleton eying her with light in his eye she did not like. She heard the word *breeches* whispered around the room, usually with sidelong glances at her, but Mrs. Hardcastle wasted no time in describing the accident that had befallen the two male actors, loudly commending Miss Drover for not allowing it to prevent the play from going forward.

Rosemary kept her eyes on the teapots and the maids distributing the cups, until the novelty of her performance appeared to wear off. By the time she was forced to join the guests, as usual on these occasions, the women were sitting in groups chatting about domestic issues, while the gentlemen stood together, talking of horses, farming or world affairs. However, she was not to escape so easily.

"Here is our heroine!" announced Mrs. Hardcastle, and there was a round of applause.

"Jolly well done!" pronounced the General. "I must say, I didn't realize it was you under that sheet until later when you appeared in those breeches. They never looked better, I dare say!"

The General obviously thought his social standing was so unimpeachable that he could say what he liked. There was a slightly embarrassed murmur from most of the gentlemen, though Mr. Pendleton was heard to mutter "hear, hear," and the ladies had the grace at look at the floor, all except Mrs. Mannering, who looked at Rosemary with patent dislike.

"It's lucky Rosemary knew all the lines, because she wrote the play," cried Marianne, instinctively recognizing that her companion somehow needed protection, "and she worked out so quickly how she could play all the missing parts. I think she's amazing!"

"And I think my fellow actors deserve most of the credit for continuing as if nothing were amiss" said Rosemary, smiling at Marianne and glad to be able to deflect the conversation from herself. "We must thank them all for their hard work and dedication, not excluding the poor young gentlemen who are lying abed and missed it all. Tell us, Mrs. Hardcastle, ma'am, how were they going on when you left?"

Thus she diverted the conversation, and his lordship, who was not enjoying the oblique references to the charms of a woman he unaccountably was beginning to think of as his own, took the opportunity to announce that sherry or Madeira was available for the gentlemen who preferred that to tea. He was certainly one of them.

Chapter Ten

One day at the beginning of the summer, Mrs. Hardcastle mentioned she was taking Mariah into Tunbridge Wells to look for materials for lighter gowns. Rosemary had received her new quarterly salary, and Marianne her allowance, so they were both feeling quite well off. Marianne begged that they might go along. Mrs. Hardcastle willingly agreed and told them she had a "treasure" in the village who made all her gowns and she would be glad to take them to her. However, since their kind friend favored gowns that were at least fifteen years out of date, and Mariah was often clad in colors that did not become her pale complexion, Rosemary had to use all her address to persuade their neighbor that between herself and Mrs. Croft they managed very well.

In Tunbridge Wells, they were introduced to a number of delightful shops catering to the visitors who came to the little town to drink from the chalybeate spring. This had a reputation for its healing qualities, particularly for women who were said to benefit from the waters, especially after childbirth. Mrs. Hardcastle said she had tried it once or twice when she was much younger and had found it most unpalatable. One could observe the ochre color deposited around the stream and she declared that she did not like the idea of her insides turning yellow. It also had a rather unpleasant smell. Nonetheless, public coaches carried visitors there frequently from London, especially in the summer months, and after the quiet of the countryside, the town seemed to Rosemary and Marianne a teeming metropolis. They purchased several ells of sprigged muslin and colored chintz, as well as a straw poke bonnet each. His lordship's library was far better stocked than had been the case at Fairchild Court, and she had ready access to the newspaper every day, so Rosemary was spending much less on books. With her greatly increased salary, she felt for the first time in her life that she had money and to spare for such fripperies. She was rather dismayed to find that she enjoyed it and hoped she was not going to develop into one of those frivolous females who thought of nothing but their appearance.

If her appearance was generally not uppermost in Rosemary's mind, it was otherwise with the Earl. His mind constantly returned, unbidden, to the sight of her bending over in those breeches, and though he inwardly cursed himself for a fool, he found himself tracing the outline of her form when he saw her in the new cotton summer gowns.

Knowing that she read the newspaper every day, he also found himself talking to her about what they had both read.

"I see Joseph Banks has died," he remarked one evening at dinner. "I must say, I never thought much of his idea of sending convicted criminals to the Antipodes. They must surely be the principal inhabitants of the colony there and, in the long run, people it with descendants of lawless people such as themselves. Botany Bay, as I believe it is called, must be a dreadfully violent place!"

The Earl was by now accustomed to Miss Drover expressing her opinion, even if it was in opposition to his own. In this respect, she was totally unlike any of the other young women of his acquaintance, who generally murmured something like "I'm sure you are right, my lord!" He was not to be disappointed.

"Do you think, then," replied Rosemary, "that convicts are vicious by nature rather than by circumstance, and that they must inevitably pass that nature on to their offspring? I am rather of the opinion that it is often society that makes men bad, rather than some innate characteristic. I understand that Sir Joseph himself lived in Botany Bay for some time, so it can't be so dreadful."

"Perhaps you are right. I should have asked his opinion on the matter." He mused for a moment. "I went to a couple of his lectures on the plants and species indigenous to the place. He rarely mentioned the inhabitants. He was principally interested in the local vegetation, as you probably know. I remember his passing around a leaf from a tree with a most pungent aroma that one could feel descend to one's lungs. I don't remember what name he gave it, but I remember thinking it would be useful when one had an inflammation of the lungs. I have never heard of it since. But," he continued, "I am getting off the subject. Are men innately bad, or does society make them so? That is an interesting question. What do you think, Marianne?"

"Oh!" said Marianne, a little shocked at being addressed directly on such a subject. She had been wondering whether she should wear her new muslin sprigged with the prettiest little violets to the card party at the Pendletons' the following evening. "I'm sure I don't know. But," she added as the thought struck her, "when one thinks of how innocent and sweet babies are, it's hard to think they could be innately bad."

"That's what I think, too," said Rosemary warmly, smiling at her. "Or, at least, I'm prepared to give criminals the benefit of the doubt. If the judges would ask them a little about the circumstances of their life, they might not be so quick to condemn them. Men who steal may often only do so because their children are hungry."

His lordship, who was a Justice of the Peace and who often had before him local men accused by the landowners of poaching or petty thieving, wondered if he had always given them the benefit of the doubt. Perhaps they had merely been trying to feed their families. In future he would ask them why they stole. Decidedly, he thought, living with Miss Drover was disturbing in more ways than one.

At the party the following evening, the Earl was more than a little annoyed to see Maurice Pendleton pay particular attention to the governess.

"Ah!" he exclaimed as they arrived. "Here is the talented Miss Drover who has brought such elevation to our poor society!" He not only made her a marvelous leg but also kissed her hand in a manner that was more than friendly.

His lordship stiffened and had the ridiculous impulse to protest that she was *his*, that Pendleton had no right to kiss her hand, or indeed touch her at all. He was reassured to see that Miss Drover treated this effusion with cool humor and passed their host with a slight curtsey to take the hand of his wife. But as the evening progressed, he could not help but observe that Pendleton was forever at Miss Drover's side, offering her refreshment, asking if she did not feel a draught from an open window, which would be instantly closed. When cards were produced and tables made up for whist, Rosemary said she was a poor hand at cards, thereby inspiring Pendleton to immediately volunteer to sit with her to show her how to go on.

The Earl, who generally enjoyed a rubber of whist, even though that evening the stakes were so small as to be risible, was not amused by the play. He could not help stationing himself at the table with Miss Drover and her helper, and had the infelicity of watching Pendleton put his face close to Rosemary's, his hand confidentially on her arm, murmuring counsel and heaven knows what.

Then Mrs. Mannering declared she would play opposite him, but she cried with pretty alarm, he was not to discountenance her by scowling at her as he was doing at present. His lordship, who generally allowed no emotion to show on his face other than a habitual slight irony, was obliged to collect himself. The fourth was made up by the General who fancied himself a very fine player and took it upon himself to criticize everyone else, when he was not engaged in gazing down Mrs. Mannering's front.

Distracted by Pendleton's whispering, Mrs. Mannering's shrill cries of dismay when she made a mistake, and the General's violent expostulations, the Earl found it hard to concentrate. He lost a few hands that he should have won and ended up actually owing money to Rosemary. She blushed and refused to accept it, on the grounds that she would not have won it without help, and indeed, though she did not say so, she was fairly sure Pendleton had cheated by looking at the opponents' cards on his frequent forays to bring her lemonade, move the candles and open or close the windows.

They were both heartily glad when the cards were put away and dear Miss Drover was called upon to play the piano. She had foreseen this eventuality, and determined not to sit in the limelight, had coached Marianne, Mariah, and the twins in a number of ballads. They made a very pretty sight, the four young ladies in their party best, singing charming songs about love and loss and love again; the Mamas were delighted and the gentlemen amused. The General went so far as to declare that, "Demmit, there could not be four prettier gels in the county." Everyone passed into supper in high good humor, all except his lordship, who had been beaten to the piano to turn Miss Drover's pages by the ubiquitous Pendleton.

"Uncle Giles, why are you looking so stern?" asked Marianne in the carriage on the way home. "Didn't you enjoy the evening? I thought it was fun! While you were at the boring old card tables, we played lottery tickets, a thing I have never done before, and Christopher was so good at explaining it!"

"I've no doubt he was, just as I've no doubt that had you not been a personable young woman he wouldn't have bothered," replied her uncle, repressively. "It will not do, you know. Flirting with all the men in the neighborhood is behavior I shall not tolerate."

As his lordship spoke, he was aware that it was not Marianne he was referring to, but that young lady, incensed at being accused of something that was very far from her mind, protested hotly, "I was not flirting, indeed I was not! Why, Jasper and Christopher are just boys! I regard them in the light of brothers. Young men like that do not interest me in that way, I assure you!" And, unconsciously pouring oil on the cause of the flames of her guardian's ill humor, added, "You may as well accuse Rosie of flirting with that odious Mr. Pendleton. I declare, she was never more than an inch from his side!"

"Marianne!" cried the unfortunate Rosemary, who had spent most of the evening unsuccessfully trying to avoid their host, "How can you talk so? He is a married man, and was only trying to be of service to me! Flirting, indeed! I'm horrified that the idea should even have entered your head!"

But even as she said it, she was aware of how such undivided attention must have looked, so that both she and the Earl spent the rest of the drive home silently beset by the same uncomfortable reflections.

It appeared that while playing lottery tickets with her young friends, Marianne had described to them the afternoon ball she and Rosemary had attended back at home.

"It is thought to be an excellent way to practice the dances for later on when one goes to London for one's coming out," she explained. "Mrs. Killington, whose daughter Sarah was my friend at home, you know, said that there was nothing worse than a girl dancing awkwardly looking at her feet. Sarah had a dance master, of course, but lessons are not the same as a real ball. At least, it wasn't a real ball, just a few friends dancing together in the afternoon."

The other young women sighed that it sounded heavenly, and the young men agreed it was a good idea. Though they would never have admitted it, they were nervous that when the time came for them to dance at a real ball in London, their performance would betray them as country bumpkins.

"Do you think his lordship would let us have an afternoon ball, or at least, a dance party, since there aren't many of us, at High House?" asked the twins together (they were almost impossible to tell apart and usually spoke as one). "Mama says you have a lovely ballroom there, and it's a shame it's never used." They unconsciously revealed the whispered remarks of most of the people in the neighborhood.

"Yes, we've explored in there. I suppose it might be lovely," said Marianne doubtfully, "but at the moment it's dreadfully dark and everything is covered up. But I'll ask my uncle. I can't see how he would object. Rosemary would be there, after all. I suppose there's a piano in the room, though it's hard to tell with everything under holland covers. I'll go up there and look."

But the opportunity to ask his lordship did not present itself for the next few days, as he was rarely at home. He appeared to have numerous affairs to attend to all over the estate and took to leaving immediately after breakfast, eating his meals away from home and not reappearing until the ladies had gone to bed.

If the servants at High House were surprised, for the Earl was known to enjoy a quiet life when in the country and rarely dined abroad, his bailiff and estate agent were positively discomforted to find their actions supervised much more closely than usual. They began to wonder if they had in some way displeased their employer.

The truth was that his lordship was angry with himself at his visceral reaction to Pendleton's attentions to Rosemary and aware that he had come close to voicing his feelings on the ride home. He decided that putting some distance between himself and Miss Drover was imperative.

Completely ignorant of the feelings she had incited in his lordship's breast, Rosemary was nevertheless aware that she missed him. She enjoyed their discussions over the meal table and his thoughtful responses to her comments about things she read in the newspaper. Even though they generally saw little of him during the day, the house seemed empty without him in the evenings, and they stopped spending time in the drawing room after dinner, preferring to go upstairs to their rooms.

Rosemary asked for working candles and continued with her dressmaking. Marianne immersed herself in Walter Scott's *Bride of Lammermoor*, borrowed from Mrs. Hardcastle, who, luckily, did not subscribe to the view that novels were bad for unmarried women. This story just suited Marianne's romantic fantasy, being the tale of a forced, unhappy marriage and a bride who descends into madness and kills her husband. When she sighed over the fate of the poor Lucy, Rosemary prosaically remarked that she could not understand why death was preferable to marriage, even with a man one did not particularly like.

"After all," she said, "if one keeps oneself busy one need hardly ever see him. Look at us, we never see his lordship these days. If you ask me, if these romantic heroines had more to do than moon around contemplating their suffering, they would be much happier."

"Trust you to say that, Rosie! But imagine that even if you were busy, making your gowns, for example, you would always have at the back of your mind the knowledge that your dreadful husband might come in at any time and demand … well, demand his *rights*." She shuddered dramatically.

"Marianne! What a thing to think of, much less to say! And what can you know of a husband's *rights*?"

"As much as you do, I daresay, Rosie! One *hears* things, after all!"

Rosemary made no answer, but as she continued sewing, she had to admit that she knew rather little about the physical side of marriage. And as for contemplating a life in which a husband might make demands at any time … well, it was better not to think about it. But then, though she had to keep her gaze firmly fixed on her work lest Marianne see the blush that crept into her cheeks, she wondered what it would be like if the Earl were that husband, and decided it would not be awful at all.

She was to see the object of her musings sooner than she thought, and under circumstances that did nothing to calm the feelings in either breast. Marianne was often beset by cramps at a certain time of the month, and the surest remedy was a hot water bottle laid on her stomach, especially when she went to bed. That night was one of those occasions, and having at first refused the remedy saying she was already too hot, for it was a warm summer night, she finally, at around midnight, agreed that it was probably the only solution.

Over her flimsy summer nightgown, Rosemary threw her shawl around her shoulders and went quietly down the back stairs to the kitchen, not expecting to meet anyone. She carried a single candle, more to frighten the mice than to see her way, since it was almost midsummer and the sky stayed light almost all night. As she came around the bend in the stairs she gave a great start and gasped as a figure loomed up towards her, almost filling the stairway. It was the Earl. Having ridden home after staying late with his agent, he had taken his horse straight to the stables and was using this shortest way to his bedchamber.

"Miss Drover!" he exclaimed in surprise, as the person who continued to fill his thoughts appeared as if by magic before him, "What are you doing creeping around the house at this hour?"

"I wasn't creeping! I was walking quite normally down the stairs to the kitchen to fill this hot water bottle for Marianne." She held it up.

"Why on earth does she need a hot water bottle on such a warm night?" His lordship's question was not unreasonable.

"She's …er … a little indisposed. It helps with the …er, discomfort that she gets at certain … certain times," answered Rosemary, glad that the relative obscurity was hiding her blushes.

By now the Earl had taken in the full picture of Rosemary in her flimsy nightgown, the shawl slipping down as she tried to hold it, the hot water bottle and the candle, all at the same time. He was transfixed by the clear outline of her shape beneath the single layer of fine cotton and barely paid any attention to what she was saying.

For her part, Rosemary, aware that nothing more substantial than a handkerchief stood between him and her naked body, was both aroused and horrified. She could feel her nipples harden under his gaze and knew that he must see them. She made a feeble attempt to pull her shawl around her, succeeding only in dropping the hot water bottle and tipping the hot wax from the candle onto her fingers. This burned so much that she dropped the candle as well. It rolled down the stairs to his lordship's feet, extinguishing itself and coming to rest against one of his boots.

The clatter brought them both to their senses. The Earl bent to pick up the candle and Rosemary to pick up the hot water bottle. Since he was a couple of steps lower than she, as they both rose she knew that, had it been lighter, he would have been able to see clearly down the neck of her nightdress, probably to her feet. His lordship did indeed have the view she feared, though it was obscured by the shadows. It took all his willpower not to take her in his arms and kiss her, but he managed to cast his mind back to what she had said, clear his throat, and say, quite calmly, "Er... yes, of course. Well ...er, carry on. Do you want me to re-light the candle for you?"

"N...no," she replied, aware of the hammering of her heart. "I was only carrying it to frighten the mice, and I think we have made enough noise to do that!"

"In that case, Miss Drover, I shall wish you good night. I hope Marianne will be more comfortable with the hot water bottle." He bowed, as best he could in the confines of the stairway.

There was still the matter of them slipping past each other on the narrow stairwell. His shoulders were so wide they nearly touched the walls on both sides. Rosemary held her breath as he turned almost sideways and his body brushed hers as he climbed up the stairs past her. She felt the rough wool of his riding jacket on her breast and caught her breath. She stood stock still for perhaps a minute, till her heart stopped its raging beat and her breathing returned almost to normal, then went downstairs to fill the hot water bottle. It was she, not Marianne, who lay awake that night until, near dawn, she fell into an exhausted sleep.

When she awoke and went downstairs quite late in the morning, it was to the intelligence that his lordship had left for London.

"But I managed to catch him before he left," exulted Marianne, "and I asked him about the afternoon ball, or dance party, rather. He seemed to be preoccupied with something else but he said yes! We can do it! Oh Rosie, what fun! And he won't be here to spoil it with his silly talk about flirting. Honestly! As if I'd flirt with those boys! No, if I ever flirt at all it will be with a real man, and *not* Mr. Pendleton! You can have him!"

"For goodness sake, I don't want him!" replied Rosemary with a somewhat forced laugh.

In fact, she now knew, for a certainty, that there was only one man she wanted and that she must never think about it again.

Chapter Eleven

Both disappointed and thankful that the Earl was in London for the foreseeable future, and no one knew when he might return, Rosemary was able to concentrate on the afternoon dance party. This was only for the young people, of course, and nothing more was required than to prepare the ballroom, check that the piano there was in tune and make sure Marianne's gown was ready. There was no point in dancing in a day dress, as this did not give one any sense of what it was like to dance while holding a train, but she thought they might dispense with headdresses. The young men would don the traditional knee breeches and waistcoat, swallow tailed coat and as complicated a neckcloth as the individual felt capable of. This was still the only attire acceptable at Almack's, that august and conservative institution in London, accessible only by invitation, an invitation without which anyone who wished to be a member of the *ton* was doomed to failure.

As for the dances, Rosemary still had the music she had played for the ball back at home, and she had made notations of the figures the young people there first practiced, then danced. As luck would have it, the Smythes' older boy Laurence, who had been in London since coming down from Cambridge, had come home until going up for the Michaelmas term. He had spent rather too royally and now found himself without funds, or, as he expressed it, quite under the hatches until the next quarter, so rusticating suited him. He was a cheerful, happy-go-lucky soul who, especially after he had seen Marianne, declared himself ready to dance the afternoon away. He had brought with him his best friend Hugo, a rather inarticulate young man who, nevertheless, according to Laurence, was a much-sought after dance partner. This meant there were four young men and four young women, and it was possible to form a square, which many of the dances required. They would begin with the Belle Assemblée March, move on to a Quadrille, which was a long dance with a large number of possible figures. Then there would be a country dance or two, some Scottish reels, a minuet, which was still danced occasionally and allowed people to catch their breath, then a waltz. She hesitated over this, as older country people still found it shocking, but Mrs. Hardcastle said that since they were by all accounts performing it even at Almack's, she saw no objection. They would finish, as always, with the Sir Roger de Coverley.

The servants were intrigued by the idea of an afternoon dance party, and entered eagerly into the preparations. In the ballroom, the holland covers were removed, the chandeliers and furniture dusted, and the piano found to be in tune. Rosemary smiled as she remembered his lordship's remark about making sure things in his house were always in good order. It was agreed that the party would begin at two. They would dance for an hour and a half, have some refreshments, and dance for a further hour. The refreshments at a traditional evening ball would begin with white soup, but this was thought inappropriate for a summer afternoon. Cook suggested a cold collation with lemonade, which sounded perfect.

The day arrived. At the last minute, Mrs. Hardcastle sent a note to say she regretted it deeply, but could not come. She had heard that morning that an aged relative was on his deathbed and, though she did not say this, since she had expectations from his Will, she was obliged to post to his side. She was sending Mariah's maid-chaperone in her place and knew that dear Miss

Drover would understand. Since Rosemary had only wanted another adult in case of emergencies and felt quite capable of dealing with eight young people, of whom two were old enough to be called men, this did not trouble her unduly.

Marianne looked very pretty in a lemon chiffon gown with a spider gauze overdress ending in a short train which had a loop underneath for gathering onto her wrist. The gown itself was quite plain and had not taxed Rosemary's ingenuity, but the gauze overdress, in itself also quite simple, gave it a very modish air. She had put her hair wholly up for the first time, and felt very grown-up. Rosemary herself did not wear a ballgown at all, since she would not be dancing, and, in a quite plain blue cotton dress, felt very sober beside Marianne. At the last minute she put on her pearls, though in general one did not wear jewelry in the afternoon, and arranged her hair in becoming ringlets instead of braiding it over her head as she usually did during the day. The other guests arrived. Mariah wore a pink satin gown embellished with rosebuds all down the front and around the neck and sleeves. It was charming, but in truth, not a good color for her and a little overwhelming for her slight frame. The twins, as usual, were dressed identically in apple green gowns with white knots around the sleeve edges and down the skirt, which were very becoming, if only they could stop fidgeting and pulling at each other. Jasper and the other young men were all very correctly dressed for a ball in knee breeches and long tailed jackets, though Christopher had affected such high points to his collar that he could hardly turn his head.

The Belle Assemblée March, with which they began was very easy, and once the movement had been explained, everyone could perform it without difficulty. It was a nice sight to see the eight of them lined up at the end, skipping elegantly down the full length of the ballroom. The maids, peeping around the door, enjoyed it immensely and performed the steps with each other outside. Anstruther cast an indulgent eye on them and let them be.

The Quadrille, which came next, required rather more instruction. Luckily, Hugo did indeed prove to be an adept dancer and demonstrated the steps with Marianne, who had had the opportunity to dance them before. They all practiced the figures and the dance began, but not before an argument ensued as to who should dance with whom. Naturally, Jasper did not want to dance with his sister, and the giggling twins hardly endeared themselves to the college men and Christopher, who thought himself quite above their touch. But Marianne could not partner all the men at once, so it was finally agreed that the partners would change in strict rotation with every dance, no matter what.

The first half of the party passed very agreeably, with the Quadrille and the country dances. Mariah proved herself a quick learner and light on her feet, and even the twins behaved more appropriately. After the prescribed hour and a half, Rosemary called a halt, saying she needed a cup of tea and she was sure everyone else must be thirsty. The assembled company, forgetting they were supposed to be adults, acted as healthy young people inevitably will, falling upon the refreshments laid out in the dining room and devouring everything, declaring it utterly delicious. In this they were joined by Mariah's maid-chaperone, who, although she had done nothing but watch, smile and clap delightedly at the charming performance of her darling, was apparently inordinately hungry and ate everything in sight.

The refreshment break was just coming to an end when Rosemary was disagreeably surprised by the arrival of Maurice Pendleton.

"Came to see how the girls were gettin' along, don't you know," he pronounced when he had been introduced by Anstruther. "They cottoning on all right?"

Papa!" cried the twins in unison. "It's so much fun, you've no idea! We've danced all the dances, haven't we, Miss Drover?"

"Yes, you have, and very creditably, too. Your Mama and Papa should be proud of you. You've no reason to worry, Mr. Pendleton, the carriage will bring them home at the end."

"Think I'll just hang on and see some of the fun, if you don't mind, Miss Drover. Damned sight more interestin' than anything going on at home."

Since the Pendletons' baby boy was now only about five months old, one would have thought that a husband's place might reasonably by his wife's side, but this appeared not to be so. Rosemary reluctantly agreed, and Pendleton followed her back into the ballroom. He stationed himself close to her at the piano and as she began to play leaned over her, ostensibly to follow the music. Ignoring him, Rosemary ran through the melody of the first of the Scottish reels. Hugo deftly demonstrated the steps, this time, much to her blushing delight, with Mariah as his partner. Before long all eight were trying the *pas de basque*, the girls lifting their skirts to their ankles and displaying their kid slippers. Then they were skipping around to the music of swirling tartan. The reels were very popular and Rosemary was begged for a couple more before, out of breath and bosoms heaving, they simmered down to the minuet.

It was at last time for the waltz, the moment the girls had been longing for and dreading, when the men would encircle their waists. Hugo first demonstrated the steps with Marianne, who had danced the waltz before. Then, recognizing the superior claim of the college men, Jasper and Christopher took the twins, wide eyed with excitement. Laurence took Marianne firmly by the hand and Hugo returned to Mariah, with whom he had formed something of a bond. The attachment was real enough; the two were married three years later, both of them inarticulate in company but unaccountably fluent with each other. They became known as the prettiest dancers in London and were an ornament to any ball they attended.

The couples began slowly, carefully trying to match their steps, in most cases their eyes fixed on their feet.

"Look up, everyone! cried Rosemary. "It spoils the effect when you are staring at your feet! Look at each other!"

Hesitantly at first, but then with growing confidence, the couples danced, their heads up. Rosemary increased the tempo slightly, then increased it again, and again, until the partners were whirling around. Mr. Pendleton, ostensibly there to watch his daughters, paid them not one jot of attention. Instead, he leaned further over Rosemary, and, in imitation of the dancers, placed his hand in the small of her back, pressing it there firmly. The twins were shrieking with excitement and the others laughing at the effort at keeping up, all of them twirling crazily around the ballroom, when the Earl walked in.

He had been away from home for nearly three weeks, trying to put Rosemary out of his mind. He had paid court to a number of women during that time, all of them gratified by his attentions and prepared to indulge his every wish. To do him credit, his quarry were all women of experience, mostly married to complaisant husbands who themselves enjoyed a high degree of freedom. He had courted each for a few days, found her intensely boring, bought her an expensive gift and then acted as if he did not know her.

He had finally come back to High House, disgusted with London society women and even more with himself. He had heard the ringing sounds of the piano and had at once headed for the ballroom. He had of course forgotten that he had given Marianne permission for the dance party. She was right when she said he had appeared distracted on the morning of his departure. He had been beset by the image of Rosemary in the stairwell, and had hardly known what he was saying. So it was in no good frame of mind that he walked in to find the place in uproar, the young people careering wildly around the room, his ward in the arms of a man he did not recognize, and Pendleton bent over Rosemary, his hand in the small of her back in what looked like a caress.

The maids, who had been laughing along with everyone else, scattered at his approach.

"What in God's name is going on here?" he thundered, bringing Rosemary's fast-moving hands to an immediate halt.

She had been watching the dancers, aware of Pendleton's hand but paying no attention to him or it, happy that her idea of increasing the tempo had solved the problem of them all looking down. She had not noticed the Earl's entrance. But she heard his voice. Her heart leaped and her fingers stopped of their own accord. It took the dancers a moment to realize what had happened, then they, too, came to a halt, breathing heavily, the laughter dying on their lips. Marianne was the first to recover.

"Uncle Giles!" she exclaimed, running forward. "It's the dance party you said we could have! It's been such fun! We were just practicing the waltz."

"The waltz? It looked more like the capering of savages in the jungle!" And turning to Pendleton, who was, in fact, the chief object of his ire, "I'm surprised at you, Pendleton, allowing your daughters to behave like hoydens."

"Come, come, old chap," blustered his neighbor, who, much to her relief, had removed his hand from Rosemary's back, "Just a bit of fun, y'know. No harm in it. The girls were in a capital way! Nothing to get on your high horse about!"

Ignoring him, the Earl turned his attention to Rosemary, "And you, Miss Drover! Is this what you consider appropriate behavior for your charge? Dancing like a wild woman with a complete stranger?"

"Sir," said Laurence, coming forward. "I am not a complete stranger, I hope." He bowed. "Laurence Smythe, at your service, my lord."

The Earl stared at him. He vaguely remembered the Smythes had a son, but surely he was just a lad. Then it came to him. This was the other one – up at university somewhere, wasn't he? He bowed.

"Er... yes, of course. I didn't recognize you. Haven't seen you for some time. Been up at ... at ..."

"Cambridge, my lord. King's." And seeing Hugo out of the corner of his eyes, shifting his feet miserably, he said "Allow me to present my friend. Hugo: The Earl of Tyndell; my lord: the Right Honorable Hugo Russell. His father is Baron Latimore." The gentlemen bowed and Hugo muttered something that might have been "at your service, my lord".

The effect of these introductions was to give everyone time to cool down. Pendleton stepped back from the piano, the couples moved apart and Rosemary announced, with greater calm than she felt, "We were in any case just at the end. The carriages will no doubt soon be here to take people home. I propose we perform the Sir Roger and say our goodbyes." She looked at the Earl, "I hope that is permissible, my lord?"

Feeling not a little foolish, both at his outburst and his failure to recognize a neighbor, his lordship nodded, curtly said "carry on," and left the room. There was a perceptible sigh of relief. Rosemary turned back to the keyboard, ran through the melody and Hugo, stammering even more than usual, explained the steps. These were completed almost in silence, the joy of the gathering completely dissolved. Marianne tried to chatter in her usual way, but no one had the heart to take her up, and soon she, too, fell silent. The party broke up with whispered goodbyes. Pendleton ushered his daughters to their carriage with an attempted heartiness, but even he could feel the weight of his lordship's displeasure and finally left with little more than a nod.

Having seen their friends off, Rosemary and Marianne walked slowly back inside arm in arm.

"It was a lovely dance party, Rosie," said Marianne. "I don't care what Lord High and Mighty says."

"He isn't *dear* Uncle Giles anymore?" said Rosemary, with a little laugh. She was suddenly feeling very weary.

"No! Not after what he said! I *wasn't* behaving like a wild woman, I was just having fun, and you are not to blame for the twins shrieking like that. If anyone should have stopped them, it was their Papa! I think it's because he never has any fun himself – probably doesn't even know what it is!"

"Oh, let's not talk about it, my love! I'm just too tired. To tell you the truth, I'm glad it's over."

"I'll tell you one person who won't be glad it's over," said Marianne confidingly. "And that's Mariah! She only had eyes for that Hugo at the end. And he seemed to like her too. He *is* a good dancer, but," she hesitated, "I just don't like boys of that age. They all seem so juvenile to me. I think an older man is *much* more interesting. Don't you think so? Not like Uncle Giles, of course. He's just an old meanie!"

Rosemary's eyes suddenly filled with tears, and she had to look down quickly, so Marianne would not see. She was thinking that a man like Uncle Giles was *exactly* to her taste, in fact, not *like* Uncle Giles, but Uncle Giles himself. She knew that she was in love with him but she also knew it was hopeless. He thought she was just a silly governess, and after her foolishness today, he was probably right. He might even turn her off, then what would she do?

"You haven't met many men at all, my love," she said, when she could control her voice. "I'm sure that one day you'll meet someone not as young as Laurence, but not as old as Uncle Giles, and like the porridge in the Three Bears story, he will be Just Right!"

Marianne laughed, "Like you, my lovely Rosie," she said, "You are Just Right – and you're much nicer than porridge!"

Rosemary laughed too, though the tears still hung on the end of her lashes. "Thank you!" she said.

Chapter Twelve

When she got to her bedchamber, Rosemary sank gratefully onto her bed and closed her eyes and did not wake up until over an hour later when Marianne came in to see if she should put her ballgown back on for dinner. She had taken it off when she lay on her bed to read.

"It's so pretty and I don't know when I shall wear it again. Uncle Giles will probably refuse to let me go to any balls and he certainly won't have another one here!"

"Don't be silly! Of course you shall wear it again. But I think you should slip on another of your dinner gowns. You'll be much more comfortable not having to deal with that train." She sat up. "Talking of gowns, I fell asleep in mine and it's all crumpled. But in any case, if you don't mind, dear, I shall not come down for dinner. I'm not feeling at all the thing. Please make my excuses to your uncle and ask Anstruther to have cook send me up a bowl of soup. I'm not very hungry."

"Oh darling Rosie!" cried Marianne, "You must be exhausted! You played the piano for *hours* besides making all the other arrangements *and* sewing my dress! Here, let me help you undress and get into bed!"

"No, no," replied Rosemary, "I can do very well on my own. Run along and put on your gown or you'll be late down to dinner, and heaven knows what your uncle will say to that, after everything else."

"Just let him *dare* to say anything! I shall know how to respond!"

"No, please don't get into an argument with him," pleaded Rosemary, but Marianne was gone.

When Marianne explained that Rosemary was exhausted and not coming down for dinner, the Earl actually felt a sense of relief. He had not been looking forward to the critical gaze in her wide eyes. Dinner passed off quite quietly, because each of the diners was immersed in his own thoughts. Marianne was still angry with the way the dance party had ended, and was reliving the whole thing in her mind, re-casting herself in an ever more favorable light and her uncle in an increasingly cruel and domineering role. Just wait till Mrs. Hardcastle returned! What a story she would tell!

His lordship was trying to do the same thing, but with the parts reversed and Rosemary as the villain. He knew he had acted like a fool and he blamed Rosemary. His actions were reasonable, in the circumstances. She should not have let the party get out of hand! She should not have allowed Pendleton to caress her in that confiding manner! She should have … she should not have …, but here, his lordship's sense of justice whispered that there was nothing more she should have or should not have done. He knew that the basis of it all was jealousy. Goddammit!

"When you go back up, Marianne," he said, as his ward left him to his port, "please tell … er, ask Miss Drover to see me in the library at ten tomorrow morning".

The receipt of this message ensured that Rosemary did not pass a good night even though she was dead with fatigue.

The following morning, conscious she was looking hollow-eyed and wan, she braided her hair closely around her head, not letting a curl escape, put on her plainest gown, and went down to the library. Before she knocked on the door, she took a deep breath, certain that she was going to be told to pack her bags; that Marianne no longer needed a governess and she was inadequate as a chaperone.

His lordship was seated at a reading table in the window, the slope of the lawn visible behind him, descending to the ruined chapel. She thought he must have specially chosen that place to sit, since her face would be in full light facing the window, and his would be in shadow, with the light behind him. In fact, the Earl always sat there when he was reading in the library. He did, however, think Miss Drover was looking a little pale. He stood as she entered and gestured to a chair opposite him. They sat in silence for a moment.

"My lord …" began Rosemary, at the same moment as he started, "Miss Drover …"

He smiled, and in spite of herself, her heart lifted and she tried to smile back.

"Pray continue, Miss Drover,"

"My lord," she began again. "I think I know why you have asked me to see you this morning. I know you were … disappointed in my lack of control over the party yesterday and …"

This was exactly what he had thought, of course, but hearing her say it was enough for him to interrupt with, "I may have overreacted when I arrived, having … er, forgotten about the dance party."

"But I was foolish to play the waltz so fast. You see," she hurried on, "I didn't want them to look at their feet. My mother always said a lady should neither look at her face in every mirror, nor at her feet when dancing. I thought if I played fast they would forget their feet in trying to keep up with the music."

"Your mother was very wise. Nothing is more dull than a partner who keeps her eyes on the ground and is so busy counting she has no conversation. I confess I have no opinion about looking in mirrors, except to say it must be an instinct to do so."

"My mother felt it was an instinct one should try to quell. Having completed one's toilet satisfactorily in the morning, she used to say that only vanity is served by looking in the mirror after that, except if one is putting on or taking off a hat, of course."

"You told me before that your mother was the best and wisest woman you have ever known, and I begin to see why." He smiled again. "But that is not what we have to talk about. You are right when you say I was angry when I came upon you all yesterday. I was not expecting any of it, and the behavior of the young ladies did seem … hoydenish. Pendleton should tell his wife to have a talk with their daughters." And keep his hands off you, he almost added. "But it has made me realize that Marianne will need to be brought out in a year, and the society she is in here is unlikely to prepare her for that. It's all very well for her to gallop about and scream like a banshee in the country, but if she were to do it at a *ton* party, her chances would be sunk forever."

It was on the tip of Rosemary's tongue to protest that it was not Marianne who had been screaming, but she said nothing.

"I have therefore decided," continued his lordship, "to take her to London and put her in the care of a distant cousin of mine who will, with appropriate incentive, undertake to counsel her in drawing room manners. My cousin is no longer a young woman, or even a middle-aged one, but she has the entrée everywhere and the demeanor that goes with it. She will be able to show Marianne how to go along."

Rosemary's worst fears were realized. Marianne was to go to London, and her services were no longer needed. She felt tears coming to her eyes and knew she had to end this interview immediately. She stood up and forced herself to look straight at her employer.

"Yes, my lord. I shall inform Marianne directly. If you would please excuse me."

And she went swiftly to the door, only too aware that in a second the tears would be falling from her eyes. Once outside, she hurried into a little-used room that contained a small sink with vases and secateurs on the shelf above. It was the room used for arranging flowers brought in from the garden, and had the indefinable smell of green and loam. Rosemary put her head against the wall and gave way to racking sobs. She had to stuff her knuckles into her mouth to stifle the sound of her violent weeping. She wept for her lost mother and her vague, kindly father; she wept at the prospect of losing Marianne, whom she genuinely loved; she wept finally for herself and the love she knew she could never have.

When the paroxysm was over, she waited some time until she could calm her breath, then washed her face in the cold water in the little sink, drying it on the hem of her petticoat. She waited a while longer, then cautiously opened the door. There was no one in the hall. Taking a deep breath, she squared her shoulders and went upstairs to tell Marianne.

"But what about you, Rosie?" cried Marianne when she heard the news. "I don't mind going to London, but I'm not going without you!"

"His lordship didn't exactly say, but I imagine he will let me stay here until I obtain …" she had to stop a moment, to prevent her voice breaking, "I obtain another position. Mr. Pendleton has talked about my being governess to the twins, so I should have no difficulty."

"Mr. Pendleton! That horrid man? Never! I'm going to speak to my uncle!" and, before Rosemary could stop her, she was out of the door, down the stairs and hammering at the library door.

The Earl had been surprised at Miss Drover's abrupt departure, as he had been sure she would want to discuss what he had said, and probably, if he knew her, to disagree with him. She was not looking her best, he remembered. Perhaps she had the same indisposition as Marianne had had all those weeks ago. It was not easy, he reflected, living with females.

He was still thinking about it, when the hammered library door gave way to his ward, who strode in and stood in front of him, her bosom heaving, her eyes flashing, evidently in the throes of an extreme passion.

"Uncle Giles!" she cried, "I shall never go to London or *anywhere* without my Rosie! *Anywhere*, do you understand? If you try to make me stay with some ugly old woman, no matter how well-connected she may be, I shall run away! If you try to send me to some horrid school, I shall run away as well! And my Rosie will *never*, I tell you, *never*, go to work for that awful Mr. Pendleton. Have you seen how he looks at her? He positively undresses her with his eyes!"

His lordship was stunned. What was the girl on about? Whoever had said that her Rosie (his Rosie, too, he could not help but think) was not going to London with her? And work for Pendleton? Over his dead body was Rosemary going to work for that cad! How dare he undress her with his eyes? The fact that he himself had done so in the stairwell not so long ago and that the image was burned on his retina, was irrelevant.

"My dear Marianne," he said, as she paused for breath, "calm yourself. Wherever have you this mistaken notion that Miss Drover is not going to London with you? I never said anything of the sort, nor would I countenance it. Work for Pendleton?" the Earl sought words neutral enough to be spoken in front of his young ward, "There is no question of her working for Pendleton. I absolutely forbid it!" How he could forbid a woman of full age to work for whomever she chose was a question he did not even consider.

"Oh!" sighed Marianne. "Oh, thank goodness! Dear Uncle Giles! I knew you couldn't be so mean! I know you were fearfully angry, but it wasn't Rosie's fault! The twins were the ones making all the noise. The rest of us were paying attention to our steps!"

If he knew that the last part of this sentence was certainly untrue, her uncle said nothing to refute it. "I am in no way blaming Miss Drover for anything. It was a combination of over-enthusiasm on your and your friends' part, and misunderstanding on mine. Let us put it behind us. I'm sure you agree that it is best for you to finish your education in London, where you may acquire a little town bronze before being presented," He could not help himself and added, "If your precipitate behavior this morning is anything to go by, it will come not a moment too soon!" But since he said this with a smile, Marianne let it go.

"*Dear* Uncle Giles, thank you!" She ran impulsively around the desk and kissed him on the cheek, then, with a wave of her hand, left as quickly as she had come.

"Decidedly, my boy," said his lordship to himself, "you don't understand women as much as you thought you did, but one thing is for sure: when maidens take to kissing you on the cheek you are getting old!"

He sighed, and turned back to his paper, wondering what explosions lunchtime might bring.

Chapter Thirteen

Marianne came dancing into Rosemary's bedroom crying, "He didn't say you were not to come! He always meant for you to stay with me. It was all a misunderstanding!"

When her charge had run so precipitously out of the room, Rosemary had for a moment thought to follow her, but she was too tired, and too unhappy. Instead, she stood staring blindly out of the window, slowly taking the pins out of her wrapped braids, which she had made too tight and were pulling at her scalp. She pulled through the strands with listless fingers and rubbed her head with her fingertips. Her curls, released from confinement, sprang up all over and made her look ten years younger. When she heard Marianne's declaration, she turned with hope springing up in her eyes, and a smile forming on her lips.

"Oh, Rosie! You look so pretty like that! Don't wear those braids any more. We're going to London to be fashionable ladies!"

"You're sure you heard it right? Your uncle means for me to go with you?"

"Yes, he seemed surprised that we thought otherwise. And he said he absolutely forbids you to work for Mr. Pendleton! I absolutely forbid it too, and I'm the one who pays your wage, after all! You have to listen to me!"

"Of course, Madam!" Rosemary curtseyed to the younger woman with a smile. She felt as if a heavy stone had been lifted from her heart. "But don't refine too much upon the idea of being a fashionable lady. I have the sense that his lordship means you to be a very well-behaved young lady first and foremost."

"Oh pooh! Remember how rude he was about your old brown gowns? He wouldn't let you be seen in public until you had something nicer to wear. And that was only here in the country! He will surely want us both to be a credit to him in London!"

But Rosemary was thinking about the Earl's veto on her working for Pendleton, and her heart rose. He must care about her a little, if he felt so strongly about her going to another household! She did not care what she wore, so long as she could stay with Marianne and see him from time to time. He was essential to her happiness; she did not even try to deny it.

At lunch, Marianne besieged her uncle in her impetuous way with innumerable questions about London. Where would they live? What was his cousin like? Would they go riding in the park at the fashionable hour like all the other society ladies? Would they have a liveried page to bring them their letters on a cushion? Because she did not give him time to answer one question before going on to the next, the Earl did not attempt to answer at once, and managed to convey a few forkfuls to his mouth. But he nearly choked at the last question.

"A liveried page?" he spluttered. "Of course not! What century do you think we are living in? The butler will bring in the post, as normal. Where do you get these ideas, Marianne?"

"I'm afraid she has been influenced by the novels Mrs. Hardcastle lent her," said Rosemary apologetically, preempting what she was sure would be a critique of this reading matter directed at herself. But she was to be surprised.

"Well, I'm sure they make a change from Pascal and the other serious material you have her read, Miss Drover," he said, with a hint of humor in his voice. "And I imagine all the young women in London do the same thing. But if you suppose," he looked at

Marianne as he spoke, "that we are living in the last century with pomanders, perfumed handkerchiefs and black pages, you are in for a disappointment. Tyndell House is a quite ordinary town house in Grosvenor Square, with quite ordinary servants and quite ordinary furnishings. I'm afraid I favor comfort over fashion and the practical over the precious. I'm thinking of installing gas lighting and a closed cooking oven, if those are romantic enough for you!" He raised an amused eyebrow.

"Oh, Uncle Giles! I don't even know what a closed oven is, but gas lighting doesn't sound romantic at all! Don't you think the flickering of candlelight is much nicer?"

She was a little surprised when the other two people at the table suddenly found their luncheon plates so fascinating and addressed themselves exclusively to what was on them. But being still almost as much a child as a young lady, she, too, was interested in her lunch, and soon forgot their strange behavior.

The move to London took place about a month later. The ladies, especially Rosemary, had a great deal more to pack up this time than the last, and his lordship was insistent that they have the maids do it.

"You must accustom Marianne to how society ladies go on," he said. "If and when you are invited to stay at one grand house or the other, you will be considered most odd if you insist on packing your own trunks."

Marianne was captivated by the possibility of invitations to grand houses, but Rosemary knew it would be their standing with the servants, rather than with the other guests, that would suffer under those circumstances. For the same reason, she took advantage of another trip into Tunbridge Wells to purchase some new and expensive chemises, silk stockings and shoes, and encouraged Marianne to do the same. Her eyes watered at the cost of these extravagances, but she knew from her mother that nothing damned a visitor more quickly than cheap or worn-out small clothes.

Tired in the end of the maids asking her whether they should pack this or that gown, she directed them to simply pack everything she possessed except the old grey-brown gowns she arrived with. In fact, she directed them to be burned. The result of this was that when her things were unpacked in London, they were found to contain the breeches, shirt and doublet that Rosemary had worn for the play in the ruins. She also found the black stocking with eyes cut out that she had used for the executioner. She had forgotten they were in her cupboard, and the maids had taken her at her word. When Mrs. Wright, the rather superior London housekeeper held these items up between her thumb and forefinger, Rosemary was obliged to tell her, with a wry smile, that they had been packed in error and belonged to someone else, so to put them away for when they returned to the country.

Tyndell House was, as the Earl had said, a fairly ordinary London townhouse. It was three stories high, with a basement where the kitchens and other domestic offices were housed. In common with many such dwellings, it was deep rather than wide, with the main staircase rising in the middle of the hall, so that at the top, one could turn back towards the front of the house, or go straight ahead to the rooms at the back. The lord and lady's rooms were, of course, in the front, overlooking the park that lay in the center of the square. The others were at the back.

This is where Rosemary and Marianne found themselves. The spacious bedchambers, like the rest of the house, had ceilings with decorative friezes and center medallions and were decorated in the typically English style of the second half of the previous century. There were comfortable upholstered chairs and inlaid tables that Rosemary recognized as probably made by Thomas Chippendale – if indeed, he ever existed. Some people now seemed to think that it was his wife who wrote his famous catalog and oversaw the making of his furniture. The four poster beds and chests were of glowing mahogany and there were corner chairs they both found charming. The upholstery and draperies were straw-colored silk and the overall effect was both elegant and comfortable. Marianne was delighted with what she perceived as London style and looked forward to dressing herself in front of the long mirrors for the innumerable soirées they were sure to be invited to.

Her enthusiasm was somewhat dimmed, though not immediately extinguished, when she met Lady Gough, the distant cousin that his lordship had chosen to take charge of Marianne's preliminary introduction into London society. She was the widow of Sir Wilfred Gough, a member of Parliament better known for the butterfly collection he travelled far and wide to enlarge than for his speeches in the House. He had caught a cold on one of his expeditions and died just over a month later from an inflammation of the lungs. His relict had settled into a sedate London existence, talking with more wishful thinking than accuracy about the significance of her husband's contribution to government and inflating his importance to a degree that would have astonished that meek, self-effacing man himself. She had the entrée everywhere but went only where she was sure her importance would be sufficiently recognized. She preferred to wait for the world to come to her, and because she had such an unassailable sense of her own importance, it did, in the form of older, equally sedate members of the *ton*, or those aspiring to be accepted into that august group. She was by nature extremely frugal and it was this that the Earl was able to turn to his own account by offering her a financial incentive to undertake Marianne's social education.

Lady Gough had one son, Raymond, now in his mid-thirties, who lived with her. He took after his mother both in appearance and temperament. He was stolid, sedentary and inclined to present his opinions as immutable truth. Both were very strict in their ideas of behavior for a girl not yet out, and of the types of social events it was appropriate for her to attend.

Into this lady's settled, unexciting circle Marianne burst like a firework. When they first went to one of her afternoon salons, she grasped Lady Gough's hand in her impulsive way, saying, "Dear Lady Gough, thank you for taking me in charge. I know we shall get along famously!"

That lady looked at her down her long, thin nose and said depressingly, "I daresay, but first we must learn not to address our elders in that overly familiar way. Stand back, girl and show me your curtsey!"

Marianne stepped back in some confusion and executed a pretty curtsey. Then she said formally, "Please allow me to present Miss Rosemary Drover, my ...er, companion."

Rosemary found herself subjected to a searching head-to-toe survey through her ladyship's lorgnette. She curtseyed, but looked the lady straight in the eye as she did it. Apparently, Lady Gough found nothing to comment upon, as she simply uttered a harrumph before turning her attention back to Marianne.

"Come here, girl," she said, and when Marianne did so, looked her up and down, saying finally, "Well, you're pretty enough and your modiste is to be congratulated. Your gown becomes you and is entirely appropriate for a girl of your age."

Since the modiste in question had been Rosemary, Marianne glanced at her companion with a humorous lift to her eyebrows, but said nothing.

"Well," continued the formidable matron, "something can no doubt be done with you, I suppose. Sit down here and talk to me." She indicated with her fan the place next to her on the settee." She totally ignored Rosemary.

Finding herself excluded, Rosemary took a seat against the wall and watched events unfold. She could see Marianne chattering in her artless style and her ladyship's back becoming straighter and straighter as she appeared to retreat before the flow of the younger woman's conversation.

At last she announced, "My dear Marianne, when someone asks you how long you have been in London and where you came from, you do not answer with this flood of speech. A few sentences will suffice. No one wants to know about the view from your chamber window or the ruins you found so charming. Nothing is more pejorative to a young woman's chances than the assumption that your interlocutor is doing anything more than being polite. I already see a sad want of decorum in your manner. You must listen more and say less!"

While Rosemary had often laughingly told Marianne that a magpie must have perched on her cradle the day she was born and she had somehow mistaken it for her mother, she only rarely hushed her chatter. In fact, she knew that her erstwhile pupil's sunny, talkative disposition was no small part of her charm. She was nearly never at a loss for words and could be counted on to converse easily with the most tongue-tied of individuals.

Rosemary found this a good quality rather than the reverse and was already beginning to think that Lady Gough might not be the best preceptress for Miss Fairchild. After the first two weeks, she was convinced she was right.

Marianne very soon chafed under the yoke of her ladyship's strictures. After a particularly trying afternoon, she wailed, "Oh Rosie! I don't think I can stand another afternoon like today! To be sitting with all those old people and to listen to them prose on about how things used to be much better when they were young! I asked that boring Miss Smith, the thin one who always wears those brown beads, whether she had ever been to the Vauxhall Gardens, and you'd think I'd asked her if she'd been to the moon! But Rosie, I've heard that they are really delightful! There are all sorts of walks and attractions. Only fancy! May said she went there on her day off and there were tight rope walkers! The Rotunda is done up in a Chinese style and at night there are thousands of lanterns, apparently!"

May was one of the maids. She had come up from High House at the same time they had and was wide-eyed at all that London had to offer.

"If it is the type of place May goes on her day off, I doubt her ladyship would consider it appropriate for you, my love," relied Rosemary, regretfully.

"Oh fudge! *Everyone* goes there, not just maids and their beaux. Please say we can visit one afternoon, Rosie! In the middle of the day it must be quite unexceptionable!"

But when Rosemary addressed herself to the Earl on the topic, he merely said to ask Lady Gough, and she knew it was hopeless.

Marianne's pleasant dream of life in London was, however, supported in other ways. Shortly after they arrived, the Earl told

Rosemary he had bought a landaulette and pair that she and Marianne could have for their exclusive use. This was an elegant little vehicle with a bright yellow body and wheels, covered with a shining black retractable awning and lined in tan leather. It was drawn by a pair of nicely matched bays. Like all his lordship's vehicles, it had the Tyndell crest on the doors. Marianne loved to be seen in it at the fashionable hour in the park, especially in the new gowns she had acquired.

The second pleasant surprise in London occurred about two weeks into their stay, when the Earl told them to present themselves at the atelier of a fashionable modiste, whom he appeared to know quite well. Both ladies were surprised that he should be on any terms at all with a dressmaker. They were not to know that over the years he had paid a number of exorbitant bills emanating from that establishment. As has been remarked before, his lordship was generous to his mistresses.

Unfortunately, Lady Gough had also been asked to meet them there, so though Marianne fell immediately in love with a beautiful lace-covered court gown displayed on a stand near the front of the establishment, she was told in no uncertain terms that her new wardrobe would not include any such thing, nor any ball gowns, since she would not be attending any functions yet that required them. Instead, she had to choose three day dresses, a walking dress and two evening gowns.

As Rosemary had surmised from her own apparel, Lady Gough did not have a discerning eye in the matter of dress. Although she had approved Marianne's simple gowns before, she at first nodded approbation at a number of models that were altogether too embellished for someone of that young lady's shapely but robust frame. The Lady favored ribbons, ruffles and bows, whereas Marianne, accustomed to being clothed by Rosemary in altogether simpler lines, found them positively funny.

"Oh, no, Madam," she laughed when the third such item was produced. "I should look a positive *antidote* in anything like that! My shoulders are too broad, indeed, for ruffles like that! I should look like nothing so much as a turkey cock!"

Luckily, the modiste herself, a very superior woman who was anxious to please the Earl as much as his ward, agreed with her. They settled in the end on quite simple gowns in lovely fabrics, some with embroidered skirts or braided hems, but nothing that would accentuate Marianne's already well-developed torso. The dressmaker then turned to Rosemary.

"We must now think about you, Miss Drover. His lordship instructed me to make a similar number of gowns for you."

When Rosemary protested, she replied, "But his lordship was most insistent. He wishes his ward's companion to be as well dressed as she. He said you might object, but I was not to take *no* for an answer!"

"Upon my word, Miss Drover!" cried Lady Gough. "That is generous indeed! More than generous, one might even say." She was wondering how she might get herself included in the Earl's largesse.

Not wanting to engage with Lady Gough in a conversation about the Earl's generosity, Rosemary simply sighed and nodded. She was then measured and examined from every angle, and the modiste sent her acolytes to bring forth another series of gowns. It was hard not to become enthused considering the different styles and then to discuss the relative merits of silk: shantung, crape, chiffon or taffeta, and wool: superfine, worsted and even felt. Cotton and muslin were useful for day dresses, of course, especially in the warmer weather. The difficulty of matching stripes and checks was considered. In the end, she chose two sprigged muslin day dresses in shades of blue, two evening dresses, one in olive green silk and one in a shimmering gold, and a walking dress in fine forest green wool. She had no idea what all this finery could cost. Between them, she and Marianne had ten gowns on order. Ten! It was inconceivable!

The Earl had been fighting to restore his habitual equanimity. He had stayed away from High House after the episode on the back stairs, determined to put Rosemary out of his mind. He had never before felt this way about a woman, and certainly not about a woman so far removed from his station in life. He had never thus far contemplated marriage but had somehow always assumed that when the time came, it would be with one of the well-bred damsels presented to him by hopeful Mamas every season. It would not be with a governess. He had never been in love, nor indeed, thought that the tenderer passions were necessary in marriage. He was sure that the emotional disturbance he was feeling would pass, like a case of the measles. He had gone back to High House at last, telling himself that it was all behind him, but the sight of her with Pendleton had resuscitated all his feelings. He could not understand himself. Then all he could think about was removing her from the man's orbit.

The plan to introduce Marianne gradually into London society had been a useful ploy to do so, but now Rosemary was living in his house, he had to force himself not to see her too often. Luckily for him, the breadth of his acquaintance in London and his membership of the Clubs where he could pass as many afternoons and evenings as he wished, meant that he was quite frequently away from home for lunch or dinner and nearly every evening. Whole days would go by without his laying eyes on the object of his fantasies. He was rather like a miser with a precious stone.

For Rosemary did indeed appear more and more like a jewel. When their paths crossed, he could see practically no trace of the dowdy governess. With her hair in ringlets around her face, her shapely figure shown to its best advantage in the expertly cut gowns and her complexion glowing in the reflection of the colors chosen for them, she seemed a different person. It was only in the cool gaze of her grey-blue eyes that he saw the woman who had disturbed the even tenor of his ways. As the days went by, the whole episode in the stairwell seemed to the Earl increasingly like a dream. Rosemary herself appeared more and more remote; they no longer discussed the news; she no longer played for him in the evenings. He heard her some afternoons practicing on the piano, but he forced himself to stay away. He was content that his jewel was under his roof. It was enough.

However, Rosemary knocked on the door of his study early one morning, when he thought both ladies still in bed. She had ascertained from Brooks, the London butler, that his lordship generally did not leave the house before eleven, having breakfasted late after an hour in Jackson's Boxing Salon. His lordship was known to have a punishing right. He muttered the permission to come in, thinking it was one of the servants, and when Rosemary entered he rose to his feet in surprise.

"Miss Drover! I thought you and Marianne still abed. I … er, I've seen little of you these last weeks. You have been often invited have you not? Is the dissipation of London to your liking?" he asked, raising an ironic eyebrow.

Rosemary looked at him with precisely the clear gaze he found so disconcerting. "To tell you the truth, my lord, no. Or rather it is not the dissipation, as you term it, but the lack of it that Marianne and I are finding so wearing."

She hesitated, then continued. "The thing is, Lady Gough seems to think that the only society suitable for us is the most staid of parties, with people much older than even myself, let alone Marianne. We have been to concerts of the dullest variety with sopranos warbling Baroque songs, incomprehensible to everyone there, I dare say. If it had been Mozart, or even the more modern works of Beethoven, it would have been better, though I confess the formal song is not my favorite type of music. And we have been to readings of poetry from obscure writers who, in my opinion, had best remain obscure, to the slowest of card parties where even my poor skills seemed outstanding, and to parties where there was no entertainment at all. Compared with what we are enduring in London, Kent seems the center of frivolity. Forgive me if I speak too directly, my lord, but you did ask."

His lordship could not help but smile at Rosemary's description of their social engagements.

"I'm pleased you find it comical, my lord, but I fear it will not remain so. Marianne is increasingly fretful and I find it difficult to support her spirits when I feel she has some reason for her depression. I have taken her to St. Paul's and Westminster Abbey, which Lady Gough finds suitable excursions. They are very fine but, in truth, hardly the sort of place a spirited young woman is likely to find very appealing. She is asking to go to the Tower, with its menagerie, and the Vauxhall Gardens, which I believe would be perfectly suitable during the day, if not at night. I feel we must make some attempt to provide her with more entertainment, or her natural liveliness will find outlets we may none of us appreciate."

The lack of daily contact with her and his ward had naturally also obscured his lordship's view of the life they were leading. He was inclined to dismiss Marianne as indulging in fits of the sullens, and to think that her companion was simply a great deal too obliging.

He therefore replied, "I am, of course, much less conversant than you with what young women may or may not find interesting, but I have every confidence that Lady Gough knows what she is about. She has lived in town for many years, after all. I do not, however, like to see you brought down by Marianne's fits. It is time she learned she cannot have it all her own way. As for her doing something untoward, I'm sure your partiality for Marianne makes you refine too much upon it. It can't be as bad as all that!"

And with that, Rosemary, making her curtsey, had to be content.

Chapter Fourteen

While the Earl had a wide circle of friends in London, one of the persons he preferred not to see in the clubs, and always avoided if he could, was Baron Clive Hutchings. They had known each other a long time, and in fact had been at Eton together. Giles had good reason to mistrust his old school mate. He was fairly sure that it was he who had snitched to the beaks when Giles had climbed out of the window one night and gone to meet a girl in the village. He knew Hutchings had seen him and could think of no one else who would carry the tale. He had had his name placed on the Bill and had received a flogging he had not soon forgotten. They had seen each other occasionally during their college years, when Giles had gone to Oxford and Clive to Cambridge. Their meetings were never cordial, though Hutchings often adopted a spurious bonhomie and claimed the other as a friend.

Their relationship had, however, hardened into solid dislike when Giles had stolen from the very arms of his would-be friend a very tasty piece of muslin that Hutchings had nurtured hopes of for some weeks. She was Becky, the cheerful, generous daughter of the innkeeper at a staging post they both used frequently travelling to and from the country. She could have her pick of any of the young bucks who came and went in and out of London.

However, she happened not to care at all for Clive Hutchings, though he was a well-made man, with smooth fair hair that had not yet shown an inclination to grow thin. He had a nice enough countenance, the only objection to it a dispassionate observer might make being that his eyes were too close together. But Becky had observed him kicking a stray dog that had shown the lack of judgement to wag its tail at him. Being a lover of most animals, both two- and four-legged, she had just told Clive to "give over and keep yer 'ands to yerself," and was struggling to free herself, when Giles, on the way back from a visit to his parents at High House, came upon them in the inn yard. He sized up the situation, leaped from his horse, dealt Hutchings a punch on the nose and carried off the fair damsel who rewarded him for his valor with a victorious romp in the hay.

Becky subsequently married the local squire, a man who had lost his wife after a long illness, and who found in her a warm, enthusiastic bedfellow and a good mother to his two young children. He regarded her previous amorous adventures as no more than training for himself, and was well satisfied.

While the Earl (as he became a few years later) never spoke openly of the affair, the ironically humorous look with which he favored Hutchings whenever he saw him, showed only too clearly that it had not been forgotten. The dislike hardened into real antipathy and the Baron (as he too became not long afterwards) vowed he would do Tyndell a disservice if he could.

He now heard that the Earl had recently brought a young ward to London from the country and thought that here might be his chance. However, it soon became clear that the young ward was not yet to be brought into society; she was being sheltered by Lady Gough. But his luck was in: he remembered a Raymond Gough from Cambridge, a stolid, humorless type who had few friends and managed to bore the breeches off any he did. A few enquiries gave him the intelligence that Raymond was a member of the Stratford Club, a low-stakes card playing establishment.

He persuaded another friend who was a member to invite him there as a guest one evening and was pleased to find Raymond at a table, just finishing a rubber of whist. Hutchings made a great show of recognizing him from "the old days" and talked about the glorious events that had marked their student life. Raymond had hardly been involved in any of them, but it gave him satisfaction to make the impression he had, when that impression was heartily supported by his new friend.

Before long, Hutchings was invited to one of Lady Gough's at-home afternoons, and in due course, Marianne found herself sitting next to a newcomer, a man with smooth fair hair, thinning it was true, but who, while not young, was nice-looking and had a good deal of address. He treated her with a mixture of avuncular teasing and flattering attention. He listened carefully to what she had to say, encouraged her to expound and appeared charmed by her conversation. He laughingly said she was a bluestocking with her knowledge of music, art and French philosophy. How could she be so enchantingly pretty, he declared, and so learned? Why, she positively frightened him! Accustomed to the repression of Lady Gough and her strictures only to talk of the most neutral subjects, Marianne blossomed, and for the first time since coming to London, enjoyed herself. That evening, she chattered happily about the afternoon's entertainment.

"Just imagine, Rosie, the Baron said I frightened him with my learning! He was funning, of course, but it was so nice to talk to someone who really *listened*! He is a most attractive man, don't you think?"

"He seems pleasant enough," replied Rosemary, with more than a little reserve. "But I wonder he spent all afternoon talking to a young woman of your age, my love, as learned as you may be!"

"But why ever should you say such a thing, Rosie? I thought you would be glad to see that you were right about a real man wanting a woman to be more than a pretty face!"

"I'm not sure I said exactly that. As I recall, our discussion was about men not wanting to marry a bluestocking. We are not talking about the Baron as a suitable *husband* for you, are we?"

"Of course not," replied Marianne quickly, then after a moment, "But if we were, would that be so bad? Don't you think he would be?"

"Certainly not!" cried Rosemary, who, for reasons that she was unable to articulate had not quite liked the Baron. "He's much too old for you!"

"But you know I like older men! I have told you so many times."

"Be that as it may, it is not becoming of you to spend so long with one particular guest at any party, and you know it. Pray do not make your preference for any one man, young or old, so marked. It is bound to be noticed."

Marianne, setting her chin in a way that Rosemary knew to be dangerous, did not pursue the subject, but she made no move to avoid the Baron over the coming weeks. For his part, he made sure he was invited to all the other dull parties arranged by Lady Gough and her coterie. With his courteous manners and handsome face, he was felt to be a welcome addition to their group. He helped the older matrons to their chairs at the concert, brought glasses of ratafia and lemonade at the intervals and picked up the handkerchiefs, shawls, programs and various other items the ladies dropped like leaves from the trees in autumn. In short, they found him a most pleasing young man and were loud in his praises.

In spite of Rosemary's remonstrances, Marianne allowed herself to be the object of his particular attentions. He was everywhere she went. He sat next to her, teasing and flattering her, asking her questions, apparently finding everything she said charming. Her only experience with the opposite sex had been the young men at High House, who were often gauche or forgetful of the little attentions that make a lady feel special. She had never had any dealings with an accomplished flirt and mistook his caressing talk for love, soon imagining his heart genuinely engaged. For her part, it was easy for her to think herself in love. His worldly wisdom, his accomplished address, his gentlemanlike attention to her, all seemed the attributes of a perfect lover.

Meanwhile, never imagining that Marianne could be entertaining such thoughts about a man she herself found oddly disagreeable, Rosemary decided it simply flattered the older man's ego to have the prettiest girl in the room prefer to talk to him than to any of the other men. Since these were nearly all even older or, as in the case of Raymond Gough, too full of their own importance to talk to a schoolgirl, Marianne's preference was hardly surprising.

Rosemary might have been more alert to this danger, had she not had her own beau to deal with. To her dismay, she found herself the object of Raymond Gough's ponderous attentions. He had at first ignored her, as he felt a governess, or companion, or whatever she called herself, entirely beneath his touch. He was as conscious of his rank as his mother. But when he found her quiet conversation both well-informed and pleasingly deferential (for Rosemary did not want to upset her ladyship by telling her son that he was wrong about most matters), he enjoyed talking with her. Then when he discovered that her father had been a vicar, also educated at Cambridge, and her mother the daughter of an ancient, though impoverished family, he found she was not so beneath his touch after all. He had been singularly unsuccessful in finding a wife. He liked pretty girls, but pretty girls, who had other choices, did not like him. Plain girls, who might have had him, interested him not at all. Here was one who was both pretty and, it seemed, available. So while Marianne was blushing at teasing remarks made by her older suitor, Rosemary was trying to find a way to depress the pretentions of hers.

Another issue that kept Rosemary from paying close attention to Marianne was that it had finally been born in upon Lady Gough that not only could Rosemary play the pianoforte, she could play better than most of the performers she had paid to entertain her guests. Never one not to take advantage of something free, she had formed the habit of asking Rosemary to play. More often than not, Rosemary agreed, if only because it kept her from having to listen to the ponderous advances of Raymond Gough. He now knew she read the newspaper daily and had taken to asking her opinion on this or that pronouncement by a government minister or head of industry. He asked, but never listened to the answer, instead pronouncing his own opinion as if it had been carried down from Mount Sinai on tablets. At first, she had tried to enter into the sort of discussion she had been used to having with the Earl, but soon gave up. His invariable answer was, "My dear, as a woman you cannot be expected to understand these matters." And just recently he had added, "It would be my pleasure to explain it all to you in private, were our ...er, relationship of a different nature."

She had pretended not to understand his meaning and had given a neutral response before changing the subject, but was still fearful that he might declare himself to her.

Had the Earl known anything of either of these developments, he would have removed both his ladies from so undesirable a situation. But he was busy. He had fallen easily into his London routine: boxing for an hour in the mornings, lunching either at home, or, more often, at his club, and attending as many of the parties and routs as he felt up to. These were becoming almost daily less agreeable as he was forced to fight off the very determined advances of Charmaine Weston, a woman he had flirted with quite markedly in the spring. She had not, in the words of the observers in the Clubs, come up to scratch before the Earl had returned to the country and had too late realized her mistake. She had just returned to the capital after spending the summer in Worthing, a town adjacent to Brighton, but much cheaper. It was also without the attractions of the better-known town. There, the Prince Regent had enlarged his summer retreat into a wonderful Pavilion and the rich and fashionable provided themselves with such entertainments as might be expected wherever such people flock together.

She had spent the summer driving between the two towns and inveigling invitations where she could. She was determined that next year, it would be Brighton or nothing, and on the arm of a well-heeled protector. The Earl of Tyndell was definitely well-heeled. She had no expectations of a wedding ring, but Tyndell besides being a handsome cavalier who commanded the best of everything, was known to give expensive trinkets to his mistresses. She had jealously observed the very pretty items of jewelry adorning the beauties he had favored with his attention not so long ago and was determined to pick up where she had left off in the spring. If his demeanor was a little forbidding at times, she felt she could work with that.

"Giles!" she said, approaching him one evening at a party, "How lovely to see you! I declare I was quite desolated when you disappeared into the country back in ... April, was it? I understand you were here for a few weeks at the end of July and then you were off again."

"I'm flattered you've kept track of my movements," he replied evenly. "I seem to have been back and forth so much this summer I've lost count of them myself. But have you been away over the summer? I don't remember seeing you."

Taking it as a good sign he had noticed she was gone, she replied airily, "Oh yes, Brighton, you know. They say the air is healthful by the sea, but I found it dreadfully windy. I'm sure my complexion will never be the same."

If she had been hoping for a compliment, for, in truth, she had never ventured outside without a wide-brimmed hat and veil, she was out of luck, "Really?" he said, scanning her face. "I see no difference. Well, perhaps your nose is a little browner than the rest."

"Oh!" she said, on the point of giving him a sharp retort, but thinking better of it, "Say it is not so! I was so careful! A brown nose! How disheartening!"

"I'm sure there are many members of the animal kingdom who do not find it so," responded his lordship, "But you must excuse me, I am promised in the card room." He bowed and moved away.

Charmaine looked after him in shocked amazement. What had he meant? He must have been funning in that ironical way of his. She would take him to task next time she saw him. It would be a good excuse to strike up a conversation. But as he walked away, the Earl was thinking of how Rosemary's laugh gurgled in her throat when she was amused. Would she have been amused by what he had just said? Probably not. She would have chastised him for his unkindness. He sighed.

Sure enough, the next time she saw him, Charmaine came straight over and taxed him with saying her nose was brown.

"For it is not!" she declared. "I stared and stared at it, and I asked my abigail. She said you must have been funning, my lord."

He was going to say something cutting, but, thinking of Rosemary, replied, "Yes, I was, but it was unkind. Pray, forget what I said."

If Charmaine thought she perceived a chink in his armor, she was wrong, for he again made his excuses and left her. So it went on, every time they were at the same event over the next couple of weeks, Charmaine would tax him with something about *brown noses*, until he became heartily sick of the whole thing and wished he had never said anything. He took to scanning the room as he arrived, and if he saw her, he would either leave forthwith, or, if it was a hostess he did not care to displease, make straight for the cardroom.

So it was that, a week or so later, making his escape from a rout to which he had been invited but where he had espied Charmaine and managed to leave before she saw him, he decided to call in at Lady Gough's. He knew she was having a small party that evening but he did not know that Rosemary had been asked to play the piano. Whenever she played, Raymond Gough stationed himself beside her, with the false assertion that he could turn her pages. But since his knowledge of musical notation was slight, to say the best, he was useless to her. She still had to turn the pages herself, or worse, stop him from turning them at the wrong moment.

When the Earl came in, he was conscious of two things. First, that Rosemary was not enjoying having Raymond Gough breathing down her neck, and second that his ward was in rapt conversation with a man he knew to be his enemy. He disliked seeing Hutchings sitting next to Marianne, but his heart told him his first duty was to rescue Rosemary. He made his way to the piano.

"Gough, your mother has asked me to beg you to assist her with something. I know not what, but she seems to need you urgently. I can take over turning Miss Drover's pages."

A quick look at his mother did not give Raymond the impression she was in need of anything, but he knew her for a tyrant and dared not disobey. He left.

"Thank you!" whispered Rosemary, as her fingers flew over the keys. "His attentions become ever more pressing. I really dread that he will make me an offer!"

"An offer? What offer?" said his lordship, distracted by trying to see where Rosemary was on the page of music.

"Of marriage!" whispered Rosemary.

"What?" roared the Earl, utterly shocked and forgetting himself. Then nodding his apologies all round, with a muttered, "I turned two pages by mistake!" said in a whisper, "Marriage? To Raymond? Never!"

Rosemary's heart rose and she inwardly smiled as she had not smiled since they came to London. That was the second time he had vetoed her involvement with another man!

Neither she nor the Earl would have smiled if they could have heard the quiet conversation between Marianne and Clive Hutchings.

"I see your guardian has just arrived, Marianne, my love (for things had progressed that far between them)," he said in a low voice. "He will try to separate us. He hates me. I don't know why."

"Uncle Giles? He hates you, Clive?" whispered Marianne. "But why? I love you, so it's not possible that others should hate you!"

"But he does. I know he will forbid you to see me. Quickly, we must make plans. I'm sure he will try to keep us apart. We must decide what we are going to do. Do you trust me?"

"Of course I do! I trust you with my life!"

"Then meet me tomorrow night at the Vauxhall Gardens," he said urgently. Outside the Turkish Tent. At midnight. For the love you bear me, tell no one! Don't fail me!" He turned her palm over and passionately kissed her hand. Then he swiftly rose and, saying again in an under breath, "Don't fail me!" he left her.

At that moment, the piece Rosemary was playing came to an end, and under the sound of applause, the Baron made his bow to their hostess, mentioning something about a just remembered engagement and went out. Marianne sat, her color heightened, her heart beating so loud she was sure others could hear it.

The Earl, smiling down at Rosemary, did not see the Baron leave. When he looked up, he saw Marianne sitting bolt upright, an odd expression on her face. Her bosom was heaving. He was about to make his way to her when he found it blocked by Raymond Gough.

"My mother denies having told you she needed my assistance," he said, in a whining tone. "I believe you just wanted Miss Drover to yourself. I saw you smiling at her."

"Miss Drover is in my employ," responded his lordship, not entirely truthfully. "I was merely trying to save her from the embarrassment of asking you to leave. You were interrupting her playing." Then, his tone hardening, he continued, "It is beyond enough when someone I pay to watch over my ward is made to provide unpaid entertainment for you, and my ward is subjected to the advances of a roué almost old enough to be her father."

"The Baron is an old... friend of mine," replied Raymond, pulling himself up to his full height, which was, nevertheless, no higher than his lordship's shoulder. "He was here at my invitation."

"In that case, you should know his reputation. You and your mother have been entrusted with the care of my ward, and you have invited a known philanderer into your midst. He is not a suitable person to sit in intimate conversation with a girl of fifteen! You and Lady Gough will be hearing from me."

The Earl walked swiftly to Marianne and in a tone that brooked no disagreement bade her wish Lady Gough goodnight. Her heart still beating furiously from the assignation she had made with the Baron, she did as she was bid, without knowing whether she was on her head or her heels. His lordship took Rosemary firmly on his arm, bowed shortly to his cousin and they were all out of the door before the assembled company had any idea what was happening.

In the carriage there was silence until Marianne, who had come down to earth enough to realize the precipitate nature of their departure, and thinking she knew the whole reason why, cried, "Clive ... Mr. Hutchings, the Baron ... he said you hate him, Uncle Giles! Why? Is that why you made us leave so abruptly? What has he done?"

"We left because Miss Drover was being importuned in a way she did not care for, and because I saw you in intimate conversation with a man old enough to be your father and who I know to be of unsavory character. It's not necessary for you to know more, Marianne. Suffice it to say that if I had had any idea of his being amongst those invited by my cousin, I would never have allowed you to go there. The man is not an appropriate person for you to have in your social circle."

"What can you mean, Uncle!" Marianne's eyes flashed. "What unsavory character? The Baron has been nothing but a gentleman! He is the only person who has treated me like an adult these last weeks. He talks to me about his travels and books, and oh, all sorts of things. He likes it that I'm not just a silly girl who says yes and no in all the right places. He appreciates me!"

"I'm sure he does! He is known to have appreciated pretty girls before." Then, before Marianne could reply, continued, "You will not see him again. I forbid it. And you will spend no more time with the Goughs. I have been much mistaken in their sense of propriety."

"So he was right when he said you hated him! But I believe you are jealous because he has so much more … more *address* than you have!" exclaimed Marianne, so angry she did not care what she said. "I don't give a fig about the Goughs and the others. They are a stuffy, boring set of people and I hope never to see any of them again, but I *will* see Clive, I *will!*" And she set her chin in the stubborn fashion that Rosemary had seen many times before.

"Hush, my love," she said. "You must not talk to your uncle like that!' She was still partly in a reverie from his lordship's smile and his taking her on his arm, and wanted quiet to think it over. "You must not talk back to his lordship in such a manner. I'm sure he has good reasons for what he says. We shall discuss it later."

"There's nothing to discuss," replied the young woman, hotly.

The rest of the carriage ride was accomplished in silence. Marianne was seething with fury and madly planning how she could escape unnoticed the following evening. The Earl was furious that Clive Hutchings should vent his spleen against him by means of his ward and was almost determined to call him out. Rosemary, the only one with joy in her heart, was remembering his lordship's reaction to the idea that she might marry Raymond Gough.

Chapter Fifteen

When they arrived back at Tyndell House, Marianne did not need to be told to go to her room. She stamped up the stairs unbidden and slammed her bedroom door. She ripped off her pretty gown in a fury and pulled the pins and ribbons wildly out of her hair. She brushed her teeth in a frenzy and got into bed. She was exactly like the heroines in the novels she had read! She had a wicked uncle; she had just realized he really *was* wicked, underneath his sometimes pleasant exterior. He was trying to prevent her from seeing the man she loved. He might even send her back to High House! But she would show him! She would meet Clive the following night if it killed her! If they locked her in her room, she would climb out of the window. She could make a rope of her sheets as she had read could be done. They would probably only give her bread and water tomorrow, but who cared! Her love would sustain her. With these comforting thoughts, she slid down on the pillows and fell asleep.

The Earl watched his ward flounce up the stairs and scowled. It really was too much, he thought, for a man who had never thus far had any thought of having children, to be saddled with a baggage like this Marianne. If she was not shouting at him for some perceived injustice, she was falling in love with the last man in London he would ever see her with. What on earth was he to do with her? He would have to send her back to High House, deal with Hutchings once and for all and start the whole process of her bringing-out again next year. His heart sank.

Watching him, Rosemary could almost read his mind. "Don't worry, my lord," she said quietly, placing her hand instinctively upon his arm. "I'll talk to her, but not tonight. It's best when she gets in these moods to just let her be. I'm sure things will be better tomorrow."

They stood like that for a second. Rosemary felt her hand burning against the fine wool of his coat and the perceptible muscles beneath, and quickly withdrew it. They turned as one, and looked in each other's eyes, hers troubled, his dark and impossible to read. He seemed on the point of saying something and then he broke away.

"You were right, Miss Drover," he said, his tone not quite even. He went towards the drawing room door, then turned back and gestured for her to go ahead of him. "You said that Lady Gough and her circle were not the right persons to have care of her. I should have listened to you, and none of this would have happened." Then, remembering, "And that damned prosy son of hers would not have taken advantage of you! I am sorry."

"Oh, Raymond wasn't so bad really." Rosemary gave a shaky laugh and moved before him into the room. "I'm sure he will make some," she was about to say 'unfortunate', but stopped herself in time, "*other* woman a fine husband. I should be flattered by his attentions. He will no doubt take his place in the House like his father."

"Yes, but unlike his father who merely drew images of butterflies when there were speeches in the House, he will be the one making the speeches and boring everyone to death!" His lordship had recovered his sangfroid and laughed. Then he continued in a lighter tone, "Since I know you do not care for *fino*, Miss Drover," and as she demurred, "no, really, the expression on your face was enough to convince me. Perhaps you would like a glass of Madeira?"

He made a sign to Brooks, who was hovering in the doorway and led Rosemary to a seat by the empty fireplace. This was covered by a painted screen depicting a damsel on a swing in the middle of what appeared to be a forest, with a swain playing the lyre, evidently looking at her petticoats.

"I wonder why they always paint those types of images on fire screens," said Rosemary, rather desperately, trying to think of something neutral to say, "It's so silly really! Why is that young man playing a lyre in the middle of the forest and whoever put that swing in that enormous tree? And doesn't the maiden mind him looking up at her …" she hesitated and blushed realizing that the topic had not been so neutral, after all, "well, her ankles," she ended, rather lamely.

His lordship laughed with genuine amusement. "How unromantic you are, Miss Drover! We are supposed to dwell on the beauty and innocence of young love, not wonder about her ankles! But I must say, that fellow looks much too frail to help her descend from that swing. I wonder how she's going to get down? Perhaps that's the point. It is to remain unrequited love, she swinging forever and he strumming his instrument for all eternity."

"Poor things!" cried Rosemary, pushing the idea of unrequited love firmly away. "Even marriage to Raymond Gough might be better than that!" But then re-thinking, "No, it wouldn't! Give me the eternal swing!" *Or, please give me the Earl of Tyndell*, the thought came unbidden into her mind.

Luckily, Brooks arrived with the *fino* and Madeira. They sat on either side of the empty fireplace, looking down into their glasses, neither knowing quite how to continue.

At length, his lordship took a breath and said, "I suppose I should send Marianne back to High House until this all blows over."

Oh, no! Don't send us away! Again, the thought came unbidden, and was almost uttered. Then Rosemary came to her senses. "If you do that," she said, more calmly than she felt, "she will feel herself a persecuted heroine. It would be better to let her enjoy the entertainments London has to offer. Introduce her to some young people. Let her have some fun. But by all means, Mr. Hutchings should be strenuously discouraged from paying her his attentions. I don't care for him at all, and tried to keep them apart, you know."

"Oh, he will be, make no mistake," said his lordship his voice filled with what Rosemary perceived as real threat. "I am confident that she will be seeing him no more! But you are right, Miss Drover, we shall shower Marianne with such excitement that she will not miss him for a moment."

They sat, both with their own thoughts, finishing their glasses. When asked if she would like another, Rosemary declined.

"I am so unused to alcohol," she confessed, "I'm a little afraid of it. The Madeira is very nice, though, you were right."

"Well, you know the only way to develop a tolerance is to drink more," said the Earl, his voice almost caressing, looking at her with a smile that brought her heart into her mouth.

All at once, she felt if she stayed a moment longer, she would not be able to control herself. She could feel her breasts straining against the silk of her gown and her breath caught in her throat. She remembered the feel of his strong arm against her as he had led her out of the Gough's drawing room, and her hand burning against his coat. She stood up.

"I must go and see if Marianne has settled down. And I confess, I am very tired. If you permit, I shall go upstairs now."

He rose and walked to the door, opening it for her. As she passed in front of him, he said in a low voice, "You have been right about so many things, Miss Drover. Marianne, I … *we* are very lucky to have you with us. I hope you know that I esteem and respect you." He bowed, and for the first time, kissed her hand.

Rosemary, now totally flustered and unable to think what to say, gave a clumsy curtsey and muttered, almost inaudibly, "Thank you, my lord," and fled.

The next morning, the Earl woke early, went to Gentleman Jim's boxing studio, where he had to be prevented from nearly killing his unfortunate sparring partner, and came home to write a furious letter to his cousin, saying again what he had told her son the night before.

Tyndell House, London
Dear Lady Gough,

I write to make you aware of my very serious displeasure in your handling of the business I paid you to perform. You were to prepare my ward, Miss Marianne Fairchild, for her coming out. You thought it good to impose great restrictions on what she might and might not say and do, but meanwhile invited into your home a man known to be a serial philanderer, a man old enough to be Miss Fairchild's father, who has filled her head with nonsense.

You also took advantage of Miss Fairchild's companion, Miss Rosemary Drover, in having her entertain your guests on the pianoforte. At the same time, your son sought to attach Miss Drover's affections, so that between the one and the other, she had no chance to protect my ward herself.

It was hardly necessary for me to say that I expect no word of this to become common gossip. If I find that my ward's reputation suffers in any way from your lax oversight, you will hear from my lawyers.

Please accept, Madam, those expressions of esteem that may be appropriate in this situation.
Tyndell

Having given orders for the immediate delivery of this note and consumed an unusually fortifying breakfast, he took himself off earlier than usual to his club. He told himself it was because he did not want to see Marianne, for fear of another explosion, and he most certainly did want to see Hutchings to warn him in explicit terms to stay away from his ward. But underneath it all, he finally had to admit to himself, he was struggling with his feelings for Rosemary.

She fascinated him. There seemed to be no subject she could not talk about, but she rarely agreed with him and told him squarely when she thought he was wrong. She never flattered him. Though she had been transformed since she first came to High House, it was only in response to his directions, for she never seemed to place any importance upon her appearance. She clearly thought more about Marianne than she thought about herself … or him. Last night he had said more than he had ever intended, and her response had been to flee in confusion. Any of the other women he knew would have pressed their advantage. She had simply run away. Did she dislike him so much? Or fear him? He had no idea what her feelings were, but he now had a very good idea of his own.

Marianne was surprised, when she awoke the next day, to find her bedroom door was not locked. The maid brought in the tea as usual, and there was no sign she was to be reprimanded in any way. When she came in, Rosemary made only oblique reference to the evening before. In a strange way, Marianne was disappointed. She had been prepared to fight for her love.

"I spoke with his lordship last night," said Rosemary pleasantly, "and he agrees with me that we have been to a sufficiency of dull parties. We should see a little more of what London has to offer. Now, I am particularly keen to see the marble monuments brought back by Lord Elgin from Greece, though there is a deal of controversy over whether he did the right thing. They are in the British Museum. We'll go there this morning. But we may go somewhere of your choice this afternoon. Where would you like to go?"

Marianne immediately said, "The Vauxhall Gardens! You know I have been wanting to go for ages." It had occurred to her that it would be well to find out where this Turkish Tent was. She did not want to miss her lover in what she had been told was usually a crush.

"Very well, we shall go to the British Museum this morning and then to the Vauxhall Gardens after lunch. But Marianne, I trust that if we see his lordship, you will apologize for your intemperate speech last night. He only wants the best for you, you know, and if he says the Baron is not a suitable friend for you, it's certain he has good reasons."

"I shall *not* apologize, and I shall *not* stop talking to Clive," replied Marianne, her head held high. Here was the tyranny she knew she would have to fight, for the sake of her love. "I refuse to abandon my friend just because my uncle doesn't like him."

"I don't care for him much myself, you know that, my love," said Rosemary firmly. "But even if I did, if the Earl says *no*, it is *no*. In any case, I doubt the question will arise, as you are no longer to go to Lady Gough's. But I must insist you apologize. Even if his lordship were mistaken, you may not speak to him the way you did. It shows lack of education and breeding."

Marianne sniffed and said nothing.

In the end, the morning passed more pleasantly that might have been expected, with Marianne determined to hold herself aloof. However, her natural exuberance conflicted with her self-imposed cold demeanor, and she could not help being fascinated by the 75-yard-long frieze with its depiction of people in a religious ceremony, many on horses. But she was puzzled by the fact that, while Lord Elgin had cut them out of a temple dedicated to the goddess Athena, most or all of the figures in the frieze were men. There were three or four separate headless statues of women, including a lovely set of three, with one showing a woman reclining in the lap of another, "Just like us, Rosie!" she commented. Otherwise they seemed to be all men, clothed and unclothed.

"Why are a lot of the men naked?" she whispered at one point, blushing a little. She had never seen a man with no clothes before. "How funny it would be if men went about like that these days! One would not know where to look!"

"It might be a little chilly here in England," whispered back Rosemary, entering into the joke, but then said, more seriously, "The ancient Greeks didn't walk around naked, you know. The artists made them like that to show that they were more than normal men: gods and warriors."

"Oh. I must say, though," continued Marianne emboldened, "they look very nice naked. I like their muscles."

Before she could stop herself, Rosemary thought of the muscles she could feel in the Earl's arm the evening before and a shiver of desire ran though her. She felt the heat rising up from her neck and had to turn away and pretend to examine something else.

Luckily, his lordship was not at home for lunch, for Rosemary felt sure Marianne would make some reference to the naked statues. However, the younger girl was unaccountably subdued at the table. Rosemary guessed she was still thinking about the previous evening. In fact, Marianne had suddenly realized that she was going to disobey all the rules she had ever learned: she was going to deceive her beloved Rosie and go to meet a man in the middle of the night. She blurted out, "I do love you Rosie, you know that, don't you? No matter what."

"Of course, and I love you, no matter what."

"Really?"

"Really."

She was inordinately comforted by that one word.

Chapter Sixteen

During the afternoon, as agreed, they went to the Vauxhall Gardens. The carriage had to leave them at the gate, and after paying three shillings each they went in. In the central part of the Gardens was the Rotunda, with the orchestra placement on the balcony and the famous lake and cascade illusion. That spectacular scene was only on at night and in the light of day it looked somewhat dull and dusty. There were a number of alcoves on either side, painted with pastoral or fairy-tale scenes, in which tables and chairs were set up for people to enjoy the many foods and drinks on sale. The menu was displayed on rectangular cards set on the square lamp posts. As it was the afternoon, some of the alcoves were occupied by ladies enjoying their tea.

These central attractions were set out in a square, and they walked around all four sides before wandering to the Great South Drive, one of the long walkways bordered by fragrant shrubs and trees leading to other edifices such as a Greek temple. Odd sights met their eyes as they wandered: a man on great high stilts walking around as coolly as if he were on the ground, doffing his hat to all the ladies; a woman with a fantastic purple wig parading a pair of poodles dyed the same color; a contortionist with his heels over his shoulders, drinking a cup of tea held in his gloved feet.

It was an amazing place, and normally Marianne would have been pulling her hither and thither, chattering like a magpie. But that afternoon she was quieter than Rosemary had ever seen her. She supposed the younger woman was still mulling over the events of the night before. She herself still had much to think about.

But Marianne was thinking about the night to come. She had quickly noticed the location of the Turkish Tent. It was not really a tent at all, more like a box at the theatre, but shaped like an Ottoman palace and highly decorated. If she took a hackney and had it drop her off where they came in this afternoon, she would have no trouble finding it again. But what was the name of the road in which the entrance gate stood? She would have to ask Rosemary. Then she would just meet Clive, they would talk about what to do and she would be home before anyone knew she had left.

They arrived back at Tyndell House too late for tea and both quite weary. They plodded upstairs for a short rest before changing for dinner. Before they went into their rooms, Marianne asked casually, "What was the name of the street where we left the carriage and entered the Vauxhall Gardens?"

"Kennington Street, I believe, why?"

"Oh, I just wanted to write all about it in my diary and that was one detail I was unsure of. I imagine there are other entrances. It's so huge!"

Marianne went into her room and, found a piece of paper and a pencil on her desk and quickly wrote *Kennington Street Entrance.* Then she took off her pelisse and bonnet and lay down on her bed. She fell into a reverie about her meeting with Clive. He would probably kiss her! She was both elated and anxious. But he would tell her what to do, how to persuade Uncle Giles to let them meet. Then, perhaps next year, after she came out, they could be betrothed. She would wear his ring. He would be *hers*. Her imagination went no further than that, but it was enough to cast a rosy glow over her whole future.

Rosemary's thoughts also dwelt on love, but with less optimism. As she lay on her bed in her petticoat, she thought back, as she had done all day long, to his lordship's words last night. *I esteem and respect you*. Esteem and respect. What did that mean? Did it mean love? Of course not, she chided herself. It means exactly what it says. He thinks I'm good at my job. He respects how I act as a governess and esteems my intelligence. That's all. Do I esteem and respect him? Well yes, she thought, I do. But more than that, I *love* him! I can't help it, I love him! Oh, what am I going to do? Whatever am I going to do? She lay there, pondering this unanswerable question until it was time to dress for dinner. With any luck, she thought, his lordship would not be home for dinner. That would make it much easier.

But his lordship was home for dinner. He had spent a fruitless day, trying on the one hand to put Rosemary out of his mind and on the other to find Clive Hutchings. He had sought him in all the clubs he was known to frequent, and finally went to his rooms on Clarges Street. His man had informed the Earl that the Baron was from home, and no, he did not know where he was or when he would be back. In fact, the man was skulking in his rooms, not wanting to meet the Earl, who he was sure would be looking for him. Just give him till tonight, when he would spirit Marianne away, and then present his long-time enemy with a fait accompli: a ward whose name was tarnished before she was even presented. That would put the noble house of Tyndell in a fix from which it would not easily recover. The Baron laughed mockingly to himself. And that Marianne was a tasty little piece, a little too innocent for his taste, but good enough for a few hours' diversion. He might even, after a suitable time abroad to allow the gossip to die down, return and marry the girl. Word was, she had a nice little fortune, and since no one else would have her, Tyndell would be glad to get her off his hands. Might even pay over the odds. All in all, the Baron, not unlike Marianne, but for very different reasons, was looking towards a rosy future.

Conversation at dinner in Tyndell House was at first sparse. Each of them was sunk in his or her own thoughts, until the Earl asked politely if they had had a pleasant day and if Marianne had been able to visit some of the places she had wanted to see.

Her mind completely filled with how she was going to leave the house later on and find a hackney, Marianne replied shortly, "Yes, this morning we went to see the Elgin Marbles and in the afternoon we went to the Vauxhall Gardens."

"And were they everything you had hoped they would be?"

"Yes, I suppose so," came the graceless answer.

"Upon my word, Marianne," said her uncle, a little vexed at the shortness of her response and assuming she was still angry over the night before, "You are hard to please! You chivvy Miss Drover into taking you all over London, and then when she does, you act like a spoiled child who was given candy apples instead of sugar plums!"

"I desire neither candy apples nor sugar plums!" retorted Marianne. "And I am not a child!"

"This display of bad manners rather confirms me of the opposite," said the Earl, "I hope you are not expecting to be introduced into a wider society than that of Lady Gough with such an attitude."

"I told you yesterday, I have no wish to see any of those people again, and if the rest of London is like that, I don't want to see them either."

"Marianne!" expostulated Rosemary, who had been astonished at her pupil's lack of grace, "Whatever is the matter? I thought we had fun today, did not you?"

"Yes, we did, but if my uncle thinks he is going to make me like him and be charming to a lot of his boring friends by letting me visit the sights of London, he is much mistaken!"

"Well!" cried his lordship, by now thoroughly out of temper. "Whether you like me or not is immaterial. You will do as I say, and one person you will most certainly not be charming to is Clive Hutchings! I looked for him in vain today. It's my belief he's left town to avoid meeting me. The man's a coward and a poltroon!"

"No, he is not!" screamed Marianne. "You're only saying that because you're jealous!" And she threw down her napkin and rushed from the room, slamming the door.

She ran straight up to her room and threw herself furiously on her bed, where she drummed her heels and punched her pillows, exactly like the child her uncle had accused her of being. "I hate him! I hate him!" she said over and over, until her anger gave way to tears and she sobbed as if her heart would break. At length, her tears ceased and her raging passion gave way to a calm rationality. She must run to Clive. It was clear her uncle meant to keep them apart. He was a hateful, hateful man! She would get into bed with all her clothes on, so that when the time came for her to leave, she would not have to get dressed, but simply slip on her hooded cloak and go downstairs. She would see about getting through the front hall without being observed when the time came. With the eternal optimism of youth, she was sure she would find a way.

In the dining room, the two left behind looked at each other, neither knowing what to say. Finally, Rosemary sighed and made as if to get up from the table, but the Earl stopped her.

"No, Miss Drover," he said, his tone lighter than he felt, "finish your meal. No good can come of running after her. You said so yourself, yesterday."

"I know, but I have never seen her behave like this before. She has turned into someone I don't know!"

"I am by no means an expert in teenage girls, but I suspect that what we are seeing is her first thwarted crush. She fancies herself in love, and love can make you behave quite unlike yourself … I believe," added his lordship, looking down at his plate.

Then he lifted his head and they looked at each other for a moment. The Earl seemed on the verge of speech, but the butler and a footman came in with the second course and in the flurry of serving them and removing Marianne's practically untouched plate, the moment passed. They finished their meal, talking lightly of this and that, particularly the legitimacy of Lord Elgin's actions in cutting up the Greek monument to bring it to England.

"I believe it suffered a good deal during the Ottoman occupation of Greece, and then afterwards by the Venetians bombarding the city," said Rosemary. Lord Elgin appears to have believed that they would suffer even more if left in place. In any case, he only brought half of the ruins away. The Greeks still have some left."

"Yes, but knowing Tommy Elgin and his money troubles, I wouldn't be surprised if he weren't motivated as much by financial gain as by a desire to protect the artefacts. Apparently, he himself paid for the whole cost of the removal of marbles, which went on for some years, and he was bankrupt when he finally got back to England. And the museum wouldn't pay him what he asked. He actually sued his wife's lover for a considerable sum to help tow him out of the river tick. Lives in Paris now, I think."

"Well, I thought they were marvelous and I'm glad he did what he did. I don't suppose I shall ever travel to Greece, so this is the only way I shall ever see anything of that ancient civilization."

"Yes, it's a pity that women don't generally do the Grand Tour. You, of all people, would benefit enormously from it. My mother travelled to Italy when she was first married, but all I remember her saying about it was that the shops in Paris were better than those in Rome. Oh, and that she found it fatiguing to walk up all the Spanish steps, especially when at the top all she got to see was a church!"

He was silent for a moment, "But I should not talk this way about my mother," said the Earl, ruefully. "She was good and kind to me and I loved her very much."

"We are both lucky to have had good mothers," commented Rosemary. "Poor Marianne never knew hers, so we must forgive her a great deal. And I really should go upstairs now, to see how she goes on. You will be wanting your port, in any case, so I shall wish you good night, my lord."

They both got to their feet. The Earl bowed, and, after a moment's hesitation, Rosemary curtseyed. Then she went to the door.

When she peeped into Marianne's room a few minutes later, she saw that the candles had been snuffed and the girl was obviously in bed, asleep. She closed the door quietly and went to her own bedchamber. Her mind totally on the Earl, she undressed mechanically and prepared herself for bed. But she could not sleep. She lay wide awake, staring with unseeing eyes up at the ceiling. Their friendly, neutral conversation about the Elgin Marbles convinced her that he saw her as nothing more than a well-informed female. He esteemed her as a benefit to his ward, although Marianne's behavior this evening did not speak well of the education she had received at Rosemary's hands. When he said she would benefit from the Grand Tour, it was only because he knew that, as an educationalist, she would enjoy seeing at firsthand what she had only read about in books. There was nothing personal in his remarks. He had spoken of Marianne's first crush. Was not she, who had never been interested in any man before, also experiencing her first crush? That's all it was. How foolish she was to think of love!

The object of her tortured thoughts had meanwhile decided to return to his club. He thought a hand of piquet might take his mind off Miss Drover. He told Brooks everyone else was in bed and not to wait up for him. Just leave a candle in the hall. As he walked through the streets, he was still thinking about her. His ward, on the other hand, occupied little of his thoughts. Convinced as he was that she was experiencing a girlhood infatuation, he was, finally, glad he had not been able to find Hutchings. The man was a cad, no doubt, as his disappearance from the scene proved. But with him out of the way, Marianne would soon forget him, especially if they pursued the program of seeing all London's entertainments. Miss Drover was not so easily disposed of. How easy she was to talk to! How plainly did she state her views! No simpering, no fluttering of lashes, no sighs that he was so much better informed than she! He could imagine being happy with her at the dinner table every day, and, here his thoughts turned to what he would rather not think about: how glad he would be to have her in his bed every night. He remembered her shapely outline in the candlelight of the stairwell, and the view of her as she bent over to change her costume in the ruins at High House. He became dimly aware that someone was calling his name.

"Tyndell! Are you playing or not? For God's sake man, are you in or out? Play the cards, dammit!"

He played, but was so abstracted that he found himself forgetting which cards had been played, which had been discarded and what his partner had bid. For the first time since he was just out of college, he lost badly. His friends, accustomed to his winning far more than he lost, decided he was bosky, though he did not look it.

"Go home, Giles," said one of his intimates. "Sleep it off. You're no good here. Never saw you play so badly!"

He took the advice, and with an attempt at raillery, said, "Yes, better go before I lose the farm," which his friends interpreted as another proof that he was a trifle disguised. He was one of the richest men in London and his estates covered thousands of acres. Losing a farm would mean nothing to him.

Rosemary still lay sleepless on her bed over an hour after she had come upstairs. Her room was in darkness, as she had put out the candles, looking for sleep. She suddenly heard what she thought was the creak of a door opening. Her ears strained, but she heard nothing more, and had just decided that it must have been her imagination when she was sure she heard the great lock on the front door being opened. Had his lordship returned? But no, she did not hear his firm tread on the marble of the hallway floor. Alarmed, she got out of bed and ran to the top of the stairs. No sound or shadow announced another person anywhere. She turned and sped to the windows of her ladyship's room on the front of the house. It was, of course, unoccupied, and the long, heavy curtains were pulled away from the tall windows. Looking down, she saw a figure in a hooded cloak hesitate for a minute on the pavement, then, as a hackney carriage came into view, stop it, then climb inside. As the person did so, the hood of the cloak fell back a little, and Rosemary could see a shock of fair hair in the moonlight. Marianne! Her heart in her throat, she ran to the back of the house and threw open Marianne's door. The bed was empty. With trembling fingers, she found a candle and a match. Holding the light above her, she looked around. There was no one there. The cupboard door stood open, and as she turned, Rosemary's eyes fell on a scrap of white paper on the table that served Marianne as a desk. *Kennington Street Entrance,* she read.

The implication of the address was immediately clear. Marianne had gone to Vauxhall Gardens! But why had she gone clandestinely? Surely she knew that, once he recovered from her bad manners of this evening, his lordship would probably sanction a properly chaperoned visit to the Gardens at night. Then it burst like a thundercloud over her head. The Baron! The silly girl had gone to meet the Baron. She had obviously been thinking about it all day, which was why she had been so quiet until her outburst at dinner. She must be stopped and brought home before the Earl knew she had gone!

Rosemary was still in her nightgown. Looking for a suitable dress, she opened her cupboard, where she had mechanically hung her evening gown earlier. Then her eyes fell on the shirt, breeches and doublet that Mrs. Wright, the housekeeper, had folded on one of the shelves. The executioner's cap and the feathered felt hat lay on top. If she wore the boy's clothes, bundled her hair into the stocking cap and put the felt hat on her head, she could run faster than in her skirts, and no one would find it strange. And as a boy rather than a woman without escort, she would not be subject to unwanted advances. She knew that the public in the Gardens at night was very mixed.

As quickly as she could, she donned all the apparel she had worn for the play, wound her hair into a knot, stuffed it into the stocking and rammed the felt hat on top. She knew she must look odd, but Vauxhall was the place for oddities, after all. People would just think she was in costume. She took her walking boots in her hand and crept down the stairs in her stockinged feet as Marianne must have done. His lordship's predilection for carpeted halls and stairways certainly made moving about silently much easier. Is that why he did it, she wondered.

The great front door was still unlocked, Rosemary realized. She had no key so could not lock it behind her. Pray to God they were not burgled, on top of everything else! She took the first hack that came by, driven by a burly individual who took one look at her and, when she gave the address, said, "Going to a Vauxhall masqu'rade, young master? They'll be a mort of fine doin's there, I don't doubt!"

Rosemary agreed that it would be so, and urged the driver to make haste, as she was already late. Marianne was not more than twenty minutes ahead of her, and she hoped to be able to move swiftly once she got to the Gardens.

Marianne, meanwhile, was wishing her driver would go faster. She had been delighted to be able to leave Tyndell House unobserved. Not knowing the Earl had dismissed the servants for the evening, she had expected to have to practice some subterfuge to get by Brooks, but it had been unnecessary. Then a hackney had come by almost at once, and she had congratulated herself on her efficient escape. But then he had not seemed keen on taking her up at all.

"And where would you be going, young Missy, all alone at this time of night?" he had said suspiciously.

"I am meeting ...er, friends at the Vauxhall Gardens, my good man," she had replied, with as much dignity as she could muster. "Do not stand here talking. I'm in a hurry! The Kennington Street entrance, if you please."

"More like running away from home, I shouldn't wonder," he had grumbled.

"Don't be impertinent! How can that be, when you see I have no bags with me. Now hurry up!"

He had finally clicked up his horses and they had taken off, at a far from rapid rate. She was sure it was taking longer to get there than it had earlier in the day. She had no way of knowing the time, and she sat on the edge of her seat, as if by pushing herself forward she could make the hack move faster. Then she had a pang, thinking perhaps the driver was not taking her where she wanted to go. She tried to look for landmarks as they went along, but everything looked so different at night, she could have been anywhere.

But finally, they crossed the river and she could see a great glow up ahead. Then she recognized the entrance they had used earlier. She fumbled in her reticule for the money to pay the driver. The price seemed exorbitant, and he was probably cheating her, but she had neither time nor inclination to haggle. She paid the entrance fee to a clerk who, she was glad to see, took no notice of her at all, and went in.

She gasped and blinked her eyes. The place was a blaze of lights. Hundreds of lanterns hung from the trees and from poles where there were no trees. It was unearthly! And the noise! Music sounded from the band on a balcony of the Rotunda, situated at the bottom of the square from where she stood, but it was hardly audible above the din of voices from the crowds of people milling about, or sitting in the alcoves, calling to the waiters or hailing each other. It was much more populated than it had been earlier in the day, and as she tried to hurry to her assignation, she had to make her way past couples and groups sauntering along the pathways, apparently with all the time in the world. She ground her teeth in frustration, her upbringing preventing her from simply barging past, but her desire willing her to do so. She wished she could take to the grass verge and run, but did not want to draw attention to herself, so simply pulled her hood more firmly over her head and, where she could, tapped people on the shoulder and muttered "Excuse me, please," as they often unwillingly stepped aside.

At last, there it was: the Turkish Tent. In the daytime it had looked rather gloomy and dusty inside, but now it twinkled with a myriad of lights, the veritable image of the One Thousand and One Nights Tales. She thought at first that she was too late, that she had missed the Baron. That he would not show up never occurred to her. But, suddenly, there he was, coming towards her, his hands outstretched.

"You came! My brave girl! You came!" he said, as he took both her hands.

Chapter Seventeen

With a cry of joy, Marianne fell into his arms. "Oh, I was so afraid I'd missed you!" she cried. "The hackney carriage took an age to get here, and I was sure you'd think I wasn't coming! Oh, Clive, what are we to do? My uncle says I may not see you again. He has utterly cast off Lady Gough. Not that I'm sorry about that!"

"Hush, my love, let's walk away a little, away from all these people." He led her away from the Turkish Tent, down the Grand South Drive where she had been with Rosemary that afternoon. The contortionist and the poodle lady were gone, but the man on stilts was still there, his head above the perfumed bushes and often ducking to avoid the tree branches. Marianne wondered for a moment how he could walk, with so many people milling about. But after a few minutes, Clive took her arm and turned her into a much less frequented pathway, where the lanterns were few and far between. The bushes on either side must have been of some night blooming variety, for the air was thick with their perfume. Marianne felt almost dizzy with the scent. They came to a stop and the Baron turned, taking her in his arms. This was it, she said confusedly to herself. The kiss! And so it was. He pressed his warm lips against hers and she almost swooned from the pent-up anticipation, the perfumed air and yes, hunger, for she had eaten nearly nothing since lunch. This last, prosaic notion was, of course, far from her mind, as she melted into the arms of a man who held her in a firm embrace, a man whose jacket smelled deliciously of tobacco and something else, indefinably masculine.

"I think, my dear," he said, as they broke apart, "we will simply have to go away together. I cannot lose you now. You see how your uncle hates me. He will never let us be together."

"But, Clive," she said, hardly able to think, let alone speak, "I thought ... I have nothing with me! You said to bring nothing!"

"I did not then realize how desperate our situation is. I dare not let you go back to him now. He must know you have left the house, and if you go back, he will surely lock you up, or send you away." He spoke in a low, pleading tone.

"But how will he know I have come here? No one saw me leave."

"My sweet innocent! Didn't you think how you would get back into the house?"

"But I left the door unlocked!"

"I saw him in his club tonight," the Baron lied smoothly. "He cut me, but dared not approach me. Perhaps he saw something in my eye that scared him off. Anyway, when he returns home, he will find the door unlocked and ask the servants why it is so. They will say they locked it and he will know either you or Miss Drover went out, leaving it unlocked. He is probably waiting for you now. He had been drinking when I saw him. I cannot imagine what his rage may make him do."

Marianne started with fear. Dread filled her heart and she began to tremble.

The Baron spoke gently. "Do not be afraid. Come with me now, and I will protect you. He can do nothing if you are with me."

Dumbly, she nodded. The evening had not turned out at all as she had thought it would. She had foolishly thought they would talk, watch the fireworks and go home. But Clive was right! If her uncle already knew she had gone and was waiting for her return, there was no hope of her going back without dreadful repercussions. He would lock her up, or send her away, or both!

Without realizing what she was doing, she allowed the Baron to push her through the bushes to a wider pathway, where she saw a carriage waiting. It did not occur to her that her lover must have planned this from the start, but allowed herself to be handed up into it.

Rosemary's driver had taken his passenger at his word and had put his horses along smartly, so that she arrived at the Vauxhall gardens not more than ten minutes behind Marianne. Like her pupil, she had at first been dazzled by the lights and the noise of the place, but coming to her senses, she had been able, in her boy's clothes, to run lightly along the side of the paths without causing much of a stir. She did not bother to go towards the Rotunda, since she surmised that the Baron would not want to meet anywhere under the full blaze of the lanterns. She thought he would keep to the darker pathways and therefore ran straight down the Grand South Drive until she came to the area where the less well-lit side paths branched off. Seeing no one, she, too, pushed through the bushes onto the wider lane and almost at once was aware of a dark carriage, with no lamps lit at the front, coming towards her. She pushed back against the foliage, and, as the carriage passed by, saw Marianne's unmistakable pale head inside.

The Baron must have given his driver orders to proceed at a trot rather than a gallop, as the carriage was moving quite slowly. No doubt he wanted to avoid drawing attention to it. Nor did he have any footmen on the back. Rosemary ran behind it, keeping to the grassy verge, where her footsteps made no sound, and when the carriage slowed to allow some drunken revelers to cross in front, she lightly jumped up onto the platform between the wheels at the back of the carriage. There, she made no attempt to hide herself, but stood upright as if she were part of the equipage of a gentleman with unusual tastes in the matter of footmen's livery. The Baron had drawn down the shade that covered the back window of the carriage, so no one inside could see her, and the coachman was too busy with his horses to look back. In this wise, she rode, clinging to the back of the carriage, as it left the Vauxhall Gardens, drove through the outskirts of London and into the country.

By the time the carriage had left the lights of London behind, Marianne's beating heart had calmed enough for her to wonder where she was going and who would be there to act as chaperone. She had every confidence her lover would do nothing to risk her good name. She put her hand on Clive's arm. "Where are you taking me, Clive?" she said. "Will your mother or sisters be there? You have never spoken of them, but I …"

"Mother or sisters? What are you talking about?" he interrupted with a note in his voice she did not understand. "My mother died years ago and my one sister lives in Bath. We are certainly not going there! No, my dear, we're going to the Castle, as the locals call it. My home, not too far from London, but far enough for no one to find you, at least not for tonight."

"What can you mean? Is no one from your family to meet us there?"

"No one. I fired Old Granger and his wife a couple of months ago. Terrible screech they put up, talking about how long they'd been there and owing them a pension. Where did they think I was going to get a pension from, I ask you!"

"But, but … I cannot stay with you alone like that, Clive, you know I cannot! It's not … proper. Why, everyone will think …" She could not finish the sentence.

"That's what we want them to think, isn't it? Your precious uncle will think it, that's for sure, but there'll be nothing he can do about it. He may even pay me to marry you, after that! It's perfect!" His laugh sounded unnaturally loud in the carriage.

"No!" cried Marianne, "No, it's not what I want anyone to think! I had no idea when you said we should go away that you would try to … to ruin me! Why, Clive, why? I thought you loved me!"

"I do love you, at least, I love what you can help me do. I've been trying for years to get back at Tyndell. He played me a nasty trick once, and, by God, I'll pay him back in his own coin. But I'll go one better. The wench he stole from me was no better than she should be, but you, my dear, are an innocent. A maid, and his niece besides. I'll ruin your good name and he'll be obliged to pay me to marry you. You have a nice little fortune besides, I hear. It's poetic justice, poetic justice, I tell you!"

Marianne just stared at him in the dim light of the carriage. Was this the man who only an hour ago was promising to protect her? Who had said he loved her innocence, the innocence combined with learning that he found so charming? Was he now going to destroy all that, for revenge? It wasn't possible!

"You must be mad!" she cried! "My uncle will kill you! You won't be paid to marry me, or have my fortune, because you'll be dead!"

"This is not the pages of a novel, my dear," the Baron replied silkily. "If your uncle kills me he will be tried for murder. Your reputation will still be in tatters; my death and his execution would not change that. This is not the Middle Ages, nor is it France. We do not exonerate honor killings. No, Marianne. You had best accustom yourself to the idea of being my wife – if I decide to have you – and making the best of it. You may as well start now."

He pulled her to him and pressed his mouth against hers. This time, instead of his lips being soft and warm, they were hard and parted. He pressed her head against the squabs of the carriage and to her astonishment and disgust, thrust his tongue into her mouth. She could hardly breathe but struggled with all her might. Holding her with one arm, he put his hand against her breast and pushed her against the back of the seat, so she was all but immobile.

Rosemary, holding fast to the back of the carriage which was now moving much more swiftly, could hear nothing over the sound of the horses' hooves. She pressed her ear against the painted panels and fancied that she could hear voices, but nothing more. She tried to tell herself that if Marianne were being attacked, she would surely scream, and she must hear that. Exactly what she would do under those circumstances she did not know. Jumping on the back of the carriage had been an instinct, not a plan. So she just clung there, her heart in her throat, wondering what was to become of the pair of them.

The Earl, encouraged by his friends to go home, did exactly that, arriving only a few minutes after Rosemary had left. He put his key in the lock only to find that, when he turned it, it locked rather than unlocked the door. Standing inside, he looked at it for a minute before striding to the bell rope and giving it a vigorous tug. When Brooks appeared, clad in a copious woolen dressing gown and long night cap, he was surprised to see his master standing in the hall with a look of enquiry on his face.

"Did you lock the door before retiring, Brooks?" he asked calmly.

"Of course, my lord. As always. I know you have your own key."

"Then why was it open a moment ago, when I came in?"

"That's impossible, my lord! No one else has a key to let themselves in."

"In that case, someone without a key must have let him or herself out. Since I cannot imagine any of the servants would use the front door, please ask Mrs. Wright to see if Miss Marianne or Miss Drover can shed any light on the mystery. I shall be in my study."

All a-fluster, the housekeeper came downstairs a little while later to inform him that neither of the young ladies was in her room.

"Indeed?" said his lordship calmly. "Can I have forgotten that they were invited this evening? Ah yes, I'm sorry, Mrs. Wright." He smote himself on the forehead. "I remember now something about a ridotto somewhere. It was to start later than usual – a moonlight and lanterns affair, I think. That must be it. I had forgotten it when I told Brooks to lock up. The young ladies must have not wanted to arouse him and decided to leave the door unlocked. I had intended to give Miss Drover a key, but it slipped both our minds. Please tell Brooks to go back to bed, and you do so yourself. I'm sorry to have disturbed you all for nothing."

It was not Mrs. Wright's habit to question anything his lordship said, so if she thought this a little odd, she said nothing, but bobbed a curtsey and left. No sooner was she out of sight than the Earl strode swiftly up the stairs and went towards the back of the house, where he had not been since his visitors arrived. He looked first into Rosemary's room. A faint scent, not of perfume, but of Rosemary herself, caused him to close his eyes and take a deep breath. Then he noticed a nightgown on the floor and the cupboard door standing open. He was fairly sure that Miss Drover was a woman of tidy habits and he felt a stirring of anxiety. He went quickly into Marianne's chamber, noticed the cupboard door also open and, as his eyes scanned the room, noticed the same paper Rosemary had seen not more than an hour earlier. *Kennington Street Entrance.*

The Earl had lived in London on and off since leaving Eton and was very familiar with the Vauxhall Gardens. Having outgrown its rather bawdy entertainments, he had not been there for some years. Why should Marianne have a note of the address? She had not needed it that afternoon, for the coachman would have taken them there. Then he remembered her outburst in the carriage and at dinner when he had criticized Clive Hutchings. Remembering their heads together the previous evening and the Baron's hasty departure, he now thought it highly likely that Hutchings had made an assignation with her there. Marianne had been longing to go and he had no doubt fueled her romantic ideas about moonlit meetings. Had Rosemary found out and gone with her? That would be just like her, not to stand in Marianne's way, but try to make a lesson out of it.

But if they had gone, how long ago was it? He had been in his club under two hours, so not more than that. But if he were to follow them to the Gardens now, by the time he got there, they would probably have left. He was sure Hutchings had no intention of letting Marianne come back to Tyndell House. And what would he do, if two women turned up instead of one? Would he leave them both? No. And would he take Marianne, leaving Rosemary behind to carry tales? No. He would have seen it as an opportunity to score against his old enemy by taking both the women under his protection. But where? Then it came to him:

Hutchings would take them both to his old country place. It was not far out of London. The Earl had been there, years ago. It had looked like a sort of tumble-down castle, he remembered. One of Hutchings' forebears had had a turn for the gothic and had taken a perfectly normal country house and put a tower on it. The Baron would be able to do what he liked with either of them there.

While he had been working all this out, the Earl had left Tyndell House, leaving the door unlocked, in case the ladies should return from some perfectly innocent evening and need to get in, and had walked swiftly round to the mews. There he roused the head groom and told him to get the curricle poled up with both of his matched pairs and be quick about it.

"The four of them, my lord?" exclaimed the groom, astonished. "But they're not used to that. The two pairs will make hard going of it!"

"They'll learn soon enough. Do as I say. It's …er … a wager I've made in the club. Hurry up!"

Shaking his head at the foolishness of wagers involving horses travelling at speed, which he thought his lordship had outgrown, the groom poled up the four horses as fast as he could and led them out into the yard.

"I've put the bays behind the chestnuts, my lord. I think they'll drive best that way, but they ain't used to looking at the hind end of other horses in front of their noses, so they might object, like."

"They may object, but they'll do what I tell 'em," replied the Earl grimly, as he leaped up onto the curricle and took the reins.

Within minutes, he was out into the streets, happily almost deserted at that time, across the river and thundering towards

Thornton Heath. This was the village a little under ten miles from London where the Hutchings family had its estate. It centered around a Pond, where houses were beginning to spring up as a result of its proximity to the capital and the promise of improved railway connections. The Castle, as the local population scornfully called it, for the Barons, skinflint and ungenerous to their estate workers, had never been popular locally, stood away from this developing area in a damp hollow.

Why the original Baron had chosen to build his home there, no one knew, as it was the least pleasant spot in the area: sodden and cold in winter, insect-filled in summer. The story was that the present Baron's grandfather had built the tower, enraged by the whining of mosquitoes at night and wanting to be elevated from the hollow in which his house lay. Since he had been too miserly to put more than one room in the tower, the rest of the household had to endure the insects and when the poorly installed roof began to leak and the floorboard to rot, they silently laughed at the old man's folly.

The spirited pairs of horses, as the groom had said, were not accustomed to working as a team and were restive at first. However, his lordship, well-known for his handling of his cattle and with the firm hold and calm voice they all recognized, soon brought them under control. Then he dropped his hands and let the horses have their heads. They covered the road to Thornton Heath in just over an hour. As they came into the sleeping village, the Earl reined them into a slow trot. He was a little surprised at the new building in a place he had always disliked, but rode onward, tense now that he was close to his quarry and on the sharp look-out for anything that could indicate that his ward and Rosemary were in the vicinity. As he came to the outskirts of the village to where the land fell off into a decline, he turned in the direction he remembered and was rewarded a few minutes later by the sight of a tower rising blackly out of a hollow, surrounded by trees. It was the Castle.

The road into the hollow followed the circumference of the decline first in one direction, then in the other, in a zig-zag fashion. As they descended, the tower was hidden by the trees and it was not until they arrived at the bottom that the house could be descried in the darkness. A carriage stood in front of the wide door, and as the curricle approached, the driver emerged from the interior, where he appeared to have been sleeping.

"Good evening, my man," said his lordship pleasantly, as he reined in his horses. "I believe I am in the right place? The Baron Hutchings is here?"

"That's right yer worship," came the reply. "'E's 'ere right enough."

"And his ... er companions are with him?"

"Don't know about no companions, all I saw was one wench, a-kicking and a-shoutin' she were, but 'e took her inside."

"You didn't think to help the young lady?"

"Nah! Not sticking me nose in 'is business. 'E pays me to drive, that's all."

The Earl, who had descended from the curricle while talking and had approached the man with a pleasant look on his face, now gave him the biggest shock of his life by swiftly bringing up his right fist and delivering a powerful blow to his jaw. The man's head was driven back against the panels of the coach, and he slid almost silently to the ground. Quickly, the Earl pulled the man's belt from around his waist and used it first to tie his arms behind his back and then attach him to a spoke of one of the wheels.

"Sleep well, my hearty," murmured his lordship. He looked for a minute at his horses. He hated to leave them like that, uncovered, after such a gallop, but he had no choice. He turned and strode lightly to the door of the house.

Chapter Eighteen

When the Baron had pushed her hard against the squabs of the coach, Marianne had at first struggled with all her might, but, finding that she could avail nothing against his superior strength, she stopped. Instead, she went completely limp and gave every indication that she had fainted. When Hutchings drew away from her, she slumped to one side with her eyes closed and lay there, inert.

"What the devil?" said the Baron, angry, but his voice betraying a hint of concern. "Stupid wench has probably got her stays laced too tight. She's a buxom piece, and no mistake."

Marianne was suddenly filled with the fear that he would try to loosen the stays she was not, in fact, wearing, but, after breathing over her for moment or two, he evidently thought better of it.

"You just stay there like that for now, my pretty," he said. "Better you don't put up a screech in the carriage anyway. Rest now, for by God, you won't get much rest later."

So Marianne lay there, trying to breathe evenly, wondering how long she could pretend to be in a swoon and trying to think how she could escape. At length, she allowed herself to moan and come to, sitting up with her hand to her head and saying, "Oh, I feel most dreadfully sick! I think I'm going to …" and she retched as convincingly as she could.

"Don't go casting up your accounts in the carriage, you little fool!" cried the Baron. "Put your head out of the window, for God's sake!"

Marianne unhooked the window sash and allowed the pane to drop. The rush of cool air did, in fact, feel good against her face, and she thankfully hung her head outside, heaving her shoulders in a very fair imitation of someone vomiting. From behind, Rosemary saw the top of her fair head and a rush of thankfulness flew over her as she realized the young woman was not, at least, bound or otherwise restrained inside the coach. She tried to call her name softly, but the wind and the sound of the horses drowned her voice.

Marianne drew her head back inside when she thought her paroxysm was ceasing to be convincing and when her throat was too sore to make any more retching sounds. She sat back limply against the squabs and said in a voice that was realistically hoarse, "I feel dreadful. Please don't touch me. I must just sit quietly for a few minutes." She smiled bravely but looked pitiful. If Mary Queen of Scots could face her executioner bravely, she thought, I can face this dreadful man. I shall not cry, whatever happens.

The Baron was convinced. Far from touching her, he drew away and said nothing until the carriage, having completed the zig-zag descent of the hollow, drew up in front of the house. Then he announced, in a bluff, would-be friendly voice, "Here we are, come inside and you shall have a cup of tea and be comfortable."

Marianne, however, tried to open the door on her side of the carriage and leap outside. To her chagrin, she found it locked and cursed herself for not having thought of that and unlocked it while she was hanging her head outside.

"Now, now, none of that," said Hutchings, abandoning his friendly tone. He wrapped his arms around her and bundled her bodily from the coach. She screamed and drummed her heels against his legs, having the satisfaction of feeling him flinch. Still holding her, he felt in his pocket for the key, which, with difficulty, he fitted into the lock and turned. He gave the door knob a twist, but, as Marianne renewed her struggling and kicking, put both arms around her and left the key in the lock. Stepping inside, he kicked the door shut behind him.

As the carriage had drawn to a halt, Rosemary had ducked down behind it and when Marianne began her noisy attempts to escape, dropped to the ground and ran into the trees. Once the Baron had carried Marianne inside, the coachman, muttering and sniggering to himself, had descended from the driver's platform and climbed into the carriage. From the rocking of the vehicle on its springs, Rosemary judged he was settling himself down for a sleep. She waited a few minutes and then, keeping to the shadow of the trees and then crouching as close to the ground as she could, ran to the front door and, turning the knob, let herself in. After a moment's thought, she took the key and slipped it into the pocket of her breeches. No one could now lock the door against their escape, for escape they would, come hell or high water.

Inside, there was a gloomy hall with a stairway off to the right. It was very dark, but at the top of the stairs there was the glimmer of a candle. Rosemary removed her boots and crept silently up the wooden steps. No carpeting here. Following the light, she crept to the door of what, when she peeped inside, was a very untidy drawing room. There were newspapers and empty glasses on every surface. She saw Marianne seated on a sagging sofa looking desperately around the room, and the Baron standing over her. She wished she had thought to provide herself with a stout branch or stick while she was outside, but the only thing she could see was a tarnished candelabra, devoid of candles, on a sideboard close to the door. She crept towards it, and had just picked it up when Marianne's gaze fell upon her. She opened her eyes wide. Rosemary put her finger to her lips, but it was too late. Following the direction of Marianne's startled gaze, the Baron saw her. "What the ..." he ejaculated, as Rosemary dashed towards him, waving the candelabra by one of its branches round her head and screaming like a banshee.

But she had not looked down. Her toe caught on the edge of a threadbare rug and she fell forward headlong, bringing her own forehead down on the edge of the base of her weapon. The shock of it stunned her and the pain, which followed the shock, was excruciating. The Baron did not take the time to wonder who this youth might be and how he had got there. It was clear why he had come, and it was not for his benefit. He took hold of Marianne's wrist and dragged her to one side of the room where, pulling aside a dusty, faded drapery, he revealed a door. When he opened it, a flight of steps stood ahead of them.

He thrust Marianne towards them and hissed, "Up to the tower with you, my girl. I'll deal with this boy, whoever he is, and come up there with you."

He slammed the door and locked it. Marianne, left in almost total darkness, turned around and dimly saw a set of stairs mounting to what was evidently some sort of chamber. As her eyes became accustomed to the dark, she could see an open door at the top, and the light of the pale moon falling into the room beyond. She went up, slowly, the stairs creaking at every step, wrinkling her nose at the smell of damp and decay that assailed her nostrils.

She found herself in a square room with high, narrow windows. It was, as Clive had said, a tower. There was a tumbled bed in one corner and next to it, on a round stand, an old candlestick with a stub of candle left in it. Next to it lay a striker, a device like a pair of scissors that Marianne had seen used at High House. She knew that one could produce a spark by bringing the two blades of the striker together, but she would need something that would burn easily. She could not hope to light the candle directly from the striker. She sat on the bed, hoping it was not full of mice, or worse, and realized it had a straw mattress. The cotton covering it was damp and stinking, falling into shreds, and she was able to use the striker to poke a hole in it, enabling her to pull out of few pieces of straw. The first pieces were limp and moldy, but as she enlarged the hole and pulled more, she finally came to some that were dry.

Taking a deep breath, she repeatedly brought the blades of the striker together, at first slowly and deliberately, but, when no spark was produced, with a sharper movement that produced a small spurt of light. She tried to bring it to the straw, but the spark did not last long enough. Determined now that she *would* get it to work, she lay the straw in a small pile on the round table, brought the striker as close to it as she could, and snapped it closed with increasing frustration, until, to her joy, a spark fell on the straw and it started to smoke. Carefully extracting a single straw from the pile, she held it against the smoke and blew gently on it. Her patience was rewarded: a small flame sprang up at the end of the piece of straw. Carefully, she brought the straw to the wick of the candle stub and her heart leaped as the wick lit and held a steady flame. The straw had by now burned down to her fingers, and with a start, she dropped it, where it fell against the dingy linen that hung down from the bed and lay, slightly smoking. Thinking it extinguished, she paid it no attention.

Instead, she took up the candle and held it aloft, to look around the room. The flame cast huge shadows on the walls, which, she now saw, were water-stained and moldy in spots. It was cheerless and dismal, but Marianne was elated at lighting her candle. Her success gave her courage. She would go back to the bottom of the stairs, hammer on the door until Clive opened it, and thrust the flame into his face. She would rescue Rosemary and they would run away together.

Having pushed Marianne towards the stairs to the tower, the Baron turned back to Rosemary, who had managed to get to her feet, her head aching and the world swimming before her.

"I don't know who you are or what you think you're up to," he said between his teeth, but I'll teach you to interfere with me!" and he picked her up and slung her over his shoulder.

Chapter Nineteen

The Earl, meanwhile, had arrived at the front door, and turning the knob with little expectation of anything being so easy, was surprised to find it unlocked. He heard the commotion upstairs and, taking the stairs two at a time, arrived in time to see the Baron facing him with a slim young person hanging down his back, a young person whose very shapely derriere he vividly remembered from the ruins at High House.

"Put her down, or by God, I'll kill you!" he snarled.

"*Her*, what *her*?" stammered the Baron, but seeing his lordship advancing menacingly towards him, he let Rosemary slide to her feet, when she immediately crumpled to the floor.

The Earl took one look at the contusion on Rosemary's forehead. "You unutterable coward," he cried, "striking a defenseless woman!" As the Baron tried to work out what he was talking about, the Earl took two long strides towards him, bringing forward his right fist and hammering it into his jaw. Hutchings staggered backwards and fell flat on his back. His lordship did not even glance at him. Instead, he knelt beside Rosemary and lifted her head.

"Rosie! My love! Say something!" he pleaded, and held her to his chest.

Rosemary was dimly aware of someone calling her name and tried to open her eyes, but it was not until she felt the wool of his coat and smelled the indefinable scent of the man she loved that she came fully to her senses.

"My lord! Wh... what did you call me?" she whispered.

"Rosie, my love," he repeated. "Thank God! What did that devil do to you?"

"Nothing, I tripped," she said. "I was trying to hit him with a candelabra and I tripped and hit myself instead!" She tried to laugh. "Oh, say it again!"

"Rosie, my love," said his lordship for the third time. "You are, you know. It took me a while to realize it, but you are my dearest love. I know that this is neither the time nor the place, but I implore you to marry me. I can't live without you."

"Nor I without you," she said, taking her head from the delicious roughness of his coat and looking up at him. "I tried for ages not to love you but I couldn't help it. Yes, yes, I will marry you! Oh, how my head aches!" With that unromantic declaration, she pulled off the stocking cap and her curls sprang free.

They both became aware of a hammering from behind the faded drapery.

"Let me out! Let me out," came Marianne's voice. "What are you doing to my poor Rosie? Oh Clive, I'll do whatever you want, just don't hurt my Rosie! Please don't hurt her!"

"Oh, dear, dear Marianne! She would sacrifice herself for me!" said Rosemary, tears coming to her eyes. "Don't be angry with her, my lord! She has been foolish, but she is a good girl, really she is!"

"I won't be angry with her if you call me Giles instead of *my lord*," replied the Earl with a smile. "And if you kiss me before I let her out."

So Rosemary raised her lips to her lord's, and her reaction to his putting his tongue between them was quite unlike Marianne's had been. In spite of her aching head, a surge of desire flooded her and she pressed her whole body against his. Neither was conscious of anything else until Marianne began hammering again.

"Clive! Where are you? Let me out! Please let me out! Don't hurt Rosie, I beg you!"

The Earl stood up and lifted Rosemary tenderly in his arms, placing her on the sagging sofa and brushing his lips against her sore forehead before going to the door and unlocking it. Marianne hurled herself against him, and would have thrust a lit candle in his face had he not grasped her wrist and caused her to drop it.

"I know I'm the wicked uncle," he said, bending to retrieve it, "but do I really deserve to be burned at the stake? I'm not the one who imprisoned you!" He peered up the gloomy stairs. "Where do they lead?"

"Uncle Giles! Oh, Uncle Giles, I've never been so glad to see anyone in my life! They lead to a horrid tower! It's dirty and damp and it stinks! But where did you come from? Where's Rosie? She tried to rescue me! She's so brave!"

Then she saw Rosemary lying on the sofa with her eyes shut.

"Oh, she's not dead! Please tell me she's not dead!" she rushed over to the sofa, the tears she had sworn not to shed streaming from her eyes.

Rosemary, who, in spite of her aching head, was still in the pleasant reverie from his lordship's kiss, opened her eyes and smiled.

"No, I'm not dead, my love. Thanks to your uncle. I might have been, but he knocked the Baron out cold."

At that moment, a groan came from the prostrate form of Clive Hutchings.

"Marianne!" said her uncle. "See if you can't find a pencil and some paper in this charming drawing room, or take your candle and look in the other rooms."

"I want to stay with Rosie. Can't you find some yourself?"

"Marianne!" protested Rosemary weakly, sitting up slowly. "Don't talk like that to your uncle and for once, do as you're told without an argument. Honestly, I'm beginning to think my years as your governess have been a complete waste!"

Abashed, Marianne stood up and started to look around. She found a stub of pencil that had evidently been used to mark horses in a racing paper and gave it to his lordship, who took a penknife from his pocket and sharpened it. She could not find any paper until she had the brainwave of tearing the flyleaf from a book she found lying on the floor. It was *The Castle of Otranto*, a novel she had previously devoured with passionate delight.

"Ugh!" she said, "I never want to read about maidens being imprisoned in castles again!"

"I'm glad to hear it! Now write this in your best hand," instructed the Earl. He gave her the sharpened pencil.

"I, Clive Hutchings, Baron, do hereby admit that I have this 28th day of September 1819 abducted and attempted the rape of Miss Marianne Fairchild ..." Marianne drew in her breath sharply, but kept writing as the Earl continued, "in an act of revenge against her guardian, Giles de Mornay, third Earl of Tyndell. I brought her to my home in Thornton Heath for that express purpose."

He took the paper and pencil from her and went over to where the Baron was struggling to his feet. He took the man's left arm and twisted it painfully behind his back. The Baron gave a cry.

"Sign this!" said the Earl, ignoring the other man's protests. The Baron swore but signed the document.

"Damn you Tyndell!" he muttered.

"Not before you, Hutchings," replied the Earl, pleasantly.

Then he returned to Marianne and instructed her to add to the bottom of the page and sign the following statement:

"Written by Miss Marianne Fairchild, whose signature below attests to the truth of this document."

When she had done so, the Earl folded the paper and put in in the inside pocket of his coat.

"Your presence amongst us becomes increasingly undesirable, Baron," he then said, taking the other man by the arm as before, and pushing him out of the room. "Stay here, ladies. I shall be back in a moment."

He forced Hutchings down the stairs and out the front door, over to his carriage, where the bound coachman was shaking his head like a bear. He pushed the Baron into the carriage and, holding him against the squabs said in a low voice, filled with menace, "If you ever lay a finger on anyone in my family again, Hutchings, I solemnly promise you will not live to see the morrow. And if one hint of scandal attaches to my ward about this night's work, I shall take your signed confession to the authorities. I advise you to be very careful about what you say, and to whom. I have many friends and my net is wide. Do not tempt me. In fact, I advise you to leave the country altogether. There must be other places in the world where your peculiar talents will be more appreciated than here."

He stepped back and closed the carriage door. Then he bent and unbuckled the driver from the wheel spokes.

"Ain't never 'ad no one plant me a facer like that 'afore, Gov'nor," said that gentleman, as he rose unsteadily to his feet. "And I never suspicioned it were coming, neither. Can't say as I enjoyed it, but if I've got to be milled down, I'd as lief it was one of your mettle. Good luck to yer!"

"Take the Baron back to his lodgings," responded the Earl. "I fear he's a trifle bosky. Never could hold his liquor. Here's for your pains." He threw him a coin that glinted in the moonlight, and strode back to the Castle.

"Cor, a coachwheel!" exclaimed the driver. "Now there's a gentleman it's a pleasure to do business with!"

And he mounted onto the front of the carriage and drove off, his unwilling passenger slumped inside.

Marianne and Rosemary were still sitting on the sofa, their heads together, when the Earl arrived back in the drawing room.

"Has he gone?" cried Marianne. "Oh, Uncle Giles! Please forgive me! I was never so deceived in a person in my life. Everything you said about him was true! I only went to meet him, and I never intended …"

"Yes, he's gone," interrupted her uncle, "but we can talk about it later. We should go too, if we want to get home before the servants are up. I hope you have learned a valuable lesson, Marianne. Life is not like the pages of a novel. But any anger I may have felt against you disappeared when I heard you offering yourself to Hutchings if he would spare Rosie … er, Miss Drover."

He smiled lovingly at Rosemary, who was thinking that, to the contrary, life *was* like the pages of a novel. "Even though it may have been a subterfuge to throw a lit candle in his face."

"No, I meant it!" Marianne exclaimed. "I would do anything for my darling Rosie."

"You may dance at her wedding."

She looked from one to the other. "You mean …?"

The Earl and the governess smiled at each other. "Yes," he said. "She has agreed to marry me, even though we disagree on the question of the value of education for women, and, in fact, about nearly everything else. But I have no doubt that in time she will talk me round." He took Rosemary's hand, and kissed it.

Then he snuffed the candles, and shepherded them out of the room and down the stairs. As they closed the front door behind them, Rosemary produced the key from her pocket and left it in the lock.

His lordship handed them up into the curricle. "You will be a little crushed, I fear. I brought the curricle to make as much haste as possible. It's lighter than the coach. And I'm sorry, Marianne, that I don't have four snow white chargers to pull it. I should have thought of that!" He smiled up at them both. "I think Rosie should go in the middle. You have your cloak, Marianne, but those breeches don't look very thick and I'm afraid her... well, her *sides* may be cold."

It was lucky it was dark and the moon fitful, for Rosemary's blushes were hidden. As they drove up the zig-zag side of the hollow, her head was against his shoulder and in spite of the ache, which was not improved by the lurching of the curricle over the rutted road, she had never been happier in her life.

When they arrived at the top, they looked back and Marianne exclaimed, "Look! The tower! It's on fire!"

It was true. They could see sparks flying up from the roof and the shadows of flames inside the narrow windows.

"Oh dear! The straw I used to light the candle must not have been completely dead! Thank goodness there was no one else in the house. The Baron told me he dismissed the only servants."

"We can do nothing about it now," said the Earl, calmly. "It would take too long to get back down there. All we can do is raise the alarm in the village. Let it burn. The Baron won't be needing it any more, in any case. He's going abroad."

"Good!" said Marianne. "It was a horrid place, even if it was a sort of castle. Anyway, all those novels are wrong! Being imprisoned in a tower is vastly overrated!"

The End

A Note from the Author

If you enjoyed this novel, please leave a review! Go to the Amazon page and scroll down past all the other books Amazon wants you to buy(!) till you get to the review click. Thank you so much!

For a free short story and to listen to the author read the first chapter of all her novels, please go to the website:

https://romancenovelsbyglrobinson.com

Thank you!

Please turn the page for an excerpt from

Imogen or Love and Money

An Excerpt from Imogen or Love and Money

"I heard you say quite distinctly, 'Move her out.'" The pretty young widow looked directly into his eyes without a hint of humor.

Ivo Rutherford had sighed as he walked into the foyer of the Hôtel Fleuri. It was a late evening in April, the air becoming damp as the sun set and the humidity rose from the lake. Lausanne had never been very welcoming in the spring. Lac Leman was fine and good in midsummer when the sails of small boats and the parasols of women in pretty dresses decorated its waters, but, by and large, he was beginning to wish he had never come. But, needs must. He had handed his hat and cane to the waiting liveried boy, and shrugged out of his greatcoat, letting it fall behind him with the cool assumption that it would be caught. He certainly did not look to see. He strode forward, a very tall, commanding figure, broad shouldered and with an absolute air of assurance. His entrance had been observed by a very pretty lady dressed in black.

"Bonsoir, Monsieur le Duc." The Maître d'hôtel, a short, stout man with oiled hair and a pince-nez, had come bustling from behind a shiny mahogany desk, and as he reached the visitor, he bowed, an anxious look on his face.

"Bonsoir Legrand," had come the response. "My bags are in the carriage outside. Have them brought up to my room at once."

"Mille excuses, Milor', but your accustomed chambre, she is not disponible."

"What do you mean, not available? I require it. It is my room. I am here."

"Mais non! Zat is ze problem, she is not available. A lady, a widow lady, is in occupation."

"I sent no lady, widowed or otherwise, so it is impossible one should be there, unless, of course," amended Monsieur le Duc, "you have performed this service for me. In which case I will delay my thanks until I see the lady in question." His eyes danced with amusement.

"Non, non, non!" The harassed little man, finding his English had deserted him, went into a flood of French.

The visitor listened with the light of humor still in his eyes and when the flood had run itself to a trickle, responded in an even tone, "I apprehend that a widowed lady arrived without notice, and you gave her the room that has been reserved for me these last ten summers. The solution appears obvious: move her out."

"Mais, Milor'! You 'ave nevair in ten years come before July, and now is April. You were not expected. She is installed. It is impossible to move one such as she!"

"'One such as she?' Why? What is she? The Dowager Queen? I do not wish to stand upon formality but no one else outranks me!" And, since the Maître d'hôtel appeared lost in the grades of English nobility, Milor' said it all again, in rapid French.

A clear English voice had spoken suddenly from behind them. It was the pretty lady in black. "I'm sorry to interrupt," she said, "but I believe I am the cause of all the trouble. I will gladly move into a different room."

Ivo Rutherford, Duke of Sarisbury, had turned and beheld the owner of the voice. His jaw did not drop, for he was far too well bred to allow any extreme emotion to betray him, but it is safe to say he was speechless for several seconds. The lady in front of him was indeed a widow, if her black gown, cap and gloves were any indication, but to call her the dowager anything would have been a gross injustice. She was very young, not more than her early twenties, if his Grace was any judge, and when it came to women, he was. Perhaps a little below average height, her figure was nonetheless perfect. Her black gown, high to the throat, was molded to her bosom and waist, its folds flowing over her perfect hips, flat stomach, and rounded derriere. It demonstrated the hand of an expert *modiste*. A beautiful blush glowed in her ivory skin, her wide green eyes were fringed by long black lashes and glossy curls showed enticingly around the edges of a very becoming lace cap. She had looked calmly up at him, a faint enquiry in her finely arched brows.

He immediately understood what M. Legrand had meant by "one such as she." This was not a woman one could thrust out of her bedchamber. Indeed, the bedchamber was her natural milieu. His Grace was not of a fanciful nature, but he could well imagine pages bringing her peeled grapes and bonbons on silken cushions. Doors should fly open as she approached and gravel should be smoothed before she put her foot upon it. The Duke was very far from being a romantic, in fact many of his mistresses had accused him of being cruel and hardhearted, but he felt himself springing to the defense of this vision.

"You misunderstand me, dear lady!" he had said, the smile lighting his eyes, "I meant nothing of the sort."

But she was having none of it. "As I say, I heard you. You told M. Legrand to move me out. Well, I am quite ready to be moved out. If I had known the room was reserved for someone of such elevated *rank*," she again looked him straight in the eye, ignoring the smile in them, "I would never have accepted it in the first place." She turned to M. Legrand. "If you would find me alternative accommodations, I will have my maid move my things in a trice."

"My dear Madam," Monsieur le Duc, rarely at a loss for words, was once again almost speechless. "I beg you to reconsider. I... I cannot possibly sleep peacefully in a room knowing you have been… ejected from it. Legrand should never have suggested such a thing."

But the lady was already walking away. "He did not suggest it, you did. As I say, I heard you. There is nothing to discuss. I am going for a walk and by the time I return, I expect my things to have been moved." She nodded at Legrand, "Thank you, Monsieur." She stopped and dropped a shallow curtsey. "Good evening, Your Grace." And she left.

Both men stood stock still for a moment. Legrand was the first to recover. He clapped his hands at the liveried boy and when he came forward, whispered in his ear. The boy ran off, presumably to have Madame's belongings moved. The Duke hesitated, but realizing that the situation was now out of his control, shrugged. He moved into the lounge, calling over his shoulder for a bottle of claret.

*****

If you would like to read more about Imogen and Ivo, please go to:

https://www.amazon.com/gp/product/B07ZXKVSNY

or

Regency Novels by GL Robinson

Please go to my Amazon Author Page for more information:

GLRobinson-US   GLRobinson-UK

Imogen or Love and Money Lovely young widow Imogen is pursued by Lord Ivo, a well-known rake. She angrily rejects him and concentrates on continuing her late husband's business enterprises. But will she find that money is more important than love?

Cecilia or Too Tall to Love Orphaned Cecilia, too tall and too outspoken for acceptance by the *ton,* is determined to open a school for girls in London's East End slums, but is lacking funds. When Lord Tommy Allenby offers her a way out, will she get more than she bargained for?

Rosemary or Too Clever to Love Governess Rosemary is forced to move with her pupil, the romantically-minded Marianne, to live with the girl's guardian, a strict gentleman with old fashioned ideas about young women should behave. Can she save the one from her own folly and persuade the other that she isn't just a not-so-pretty face?

The Kissing Ball A collection of Regency short stories, not just for Christmas. All sorts of seasons and reasons!

The Earl and The Mud-Covered Maiden The House of Hale Book One. When a handsome stranger covers her in mud driving too fast and then lies about his name, little does Sophy know her world is about to change forever.

The Earl and His Lady The House of Hale Book Two. Sophy and Lysander are married, but she is unused to London society and he's very proud of his family name. It's a rocky beginning for both of them.

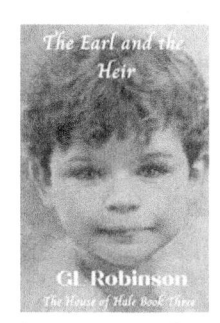

The Earl and The Heir *The House of Hale Book Three.* The Hale family has a new heir, in the shape of Sylvester, a handful of a little boy with a lively curiosity. His mother is curious too, about her husband's past. They both get themselves in a lot of trouble.

The Lord and the Red-Headed Hornet Orphaned Amelia talks her way into a man's job as secretary to a member of the aristocracy. She's looking for a post in the Diplomatic Service for her twin brother. But he wants to join the army. And her boss goes missing on the day he is supposed to show up for a wager. Can feisty Amelia save them both?

The Lord and the Cat's Meow A love tangle between a Lord, a retired Colonel, a lovely debutante, and a fierce animal rights activist. But Horace the cat knows what he wants. He sorts it out.

The Lord and the Bluestocking The Marquess of Hastings is good-looking and rich but is a little odd. Nowadays he would probably be diagnosed as having Asperger's syndrome. To find a wife he scandalizes the *ton* by advertising in the newspaper. Elisabeth Maxwell is having no luck finding a publisher for her children's book and is willing to marry him to escape an overbearing stepfather. This gently amusing story introduces us to an unusual but endearing Regency couple. The question is: can they possibly co-exist, let alone find happiness?

About The Author

GL Robinson is a retired French professor who took to writing Regency Romances in 2018. She dedicates all her books to her sister, who died unexpectedly that year and who, like her, had a lifelong love of the genre. She remembers the two of them reading Georgette Heyer after lights out under the covers in their convent boarding school and giggling together in delicious complicity.

Brought up in the south of England, she has spent the last forty years in upstate New York with her American husband. She likes gardening, talking with her grandchildren and sitting by the fire. She still reads Georgette Heyer.

Book Group Conversation Starters

1. For a long time, educated women with an interest in learning were called *bluestockings.* This was a reference to the fact that they preferred comfortable and hard-wearing garments to the silk stockings and fashionable but often flimsy clothes that society women wore. It used to be said that men were not interested in such women. Do you think that is still true today? Do men dislike clever women?

2. Marianne goes to London to learn how to get on in society. Do you think young people still need such lessons today?

3. Rosemary makes Marianne study Blaise Pascal (French mathematician and philosopher 1623-62), who is famous for his *Pensées* (*Thoughts*). One of them is that we only love people for their observed qualities, and not for themselves. Is this true?

4. The Earl says we should judge people by their actions, not by their intentions. This is a basic idea of Existentialism, an idea that reached its peak in post World War II France. What do you think?

5. This is a question that interests me greatly and I have asked before, why are Romance novels with happy endings so popular? Are they a guilty pleasure?

Printed in Great Britain
by Amazon